When is My Forever

BY

Aileen Friedman

ISBN – 13   978-0-620-55793-1

Website
http://aileenfriedman.co.za

Facebook
https://www.facebook.com/groups/353447231333743/

Twitter
@aileenlf

Editor
Franziska Annas
franziska.annas@gmail.com

Contribution
Tamara De Jager
tnsdejager@gmail.com

Cover Photo
Nadine Friedman
nadinefried@gmail.com

Cover Design
Cara Friedman
ifriedaman@gmail.com

Thank you, Lord Jesus,
for your love and mercy
and for blessing me
with my family whom I love so much.
I am truly blessed.

Phil 4:13 'I can do all things through Christ who strengthens
me.'

Table of Contents

Chapter One

Driving past the pick-up-and-go for the fifth time, I was quickly losing my patience. Dena, my mother, was supposed to have been there waiting for me. According to the person who had answered the phone at the information desk, her flight had landed forty-five minutes ago – yet there was still no sign of her. This was typical of her, so allowing myself to get irritated over her actions made my annoyance even greater.

The fact that I had to fetch her from the airport was unusual. Her fancy Mercedes-Benz S-Class was at the workshop after it had broken down five meters from our house that morning, almost making her late for her flight to Johannesburg. I'd had to get up at four o'clock to drop her off while being forced to listen to her high-pitched whining for the entire thirty kilometres. It was no wonder I'd been in a bad mood the entire day.

On my eighth round past the pick-up-and-go station, just as I had had enough and was about to leave, there she was. I almost waved and drove on, but my conscience kept me from doing so. Standing with her arm outstretched, she signalled to me as though I were a taxi and as though I would miss her.

One couldn't miss Dena. She was an attractive woman of fifty-five. With her bottle-blonde hair and all the immaculate grooming that money could buy, she looked, at least, ten years younger. Her lengthy high heels added height to her already tall frame. She had an aura about her that demanded attention the minute you set eyes on her, and she looked like she would easily devour anyone who was not careful to treat her as she expected.

She took her gracious time getting into my car while another car waited patiently for the spot we were in. Not that this concerned her at all; she was of the opinion that life was always all about her.

'Why are you late?' she accused me before she'd even greeted me.

Glaring at her, I struggled to contain my anger. I snarled through my clenched jaw that I'd been around the airport eight times and asked her what on earth had taken her so flipping long. She calmly told me about someone she had met on the plane and how they had enjoyed each other's company so much. No doubt it was a man, and, not wanting to hear any further details, I told her to keep it to herself as I was not interested. We drove in silence for the rest of the way home, thank goodness.

Dena had raised me with a nanny, Josie. My father, I had never known. Apparently he'd left us when I was two years old, and, quite frankly, if my mother had been the way she was now, I can't say I blamed him. Since he had never bothered to be a part of my life, I was not bothered to find him or find out about him. Dena was hard enough to deal with.

I had been told that I looked more like him than Dena. I had natural blonde hair, which I never missed a chance to remind Dena of when she was in one of her spiteful moods. I had green eyes and strong, rather unfeminine features. The only trait I seemed to have inherited from Dena was my height.

I completely understood that she'd had no husband to help her while I was growing up, but she'd had no shortage of partners throughout my life, too many that I cared to remember.

It had taken her a quick two years to gain a senior position in the investment company where she worked, and it was another four years until she was a director and a member of the Board. That put me at about eight years old when she became Miss Most Important Selfish Person in the World; even more so than she had been before.

When Josie finished work at five o'clock, I would go home with her to her house until my mother would eventually pick me up on her way home from work. When I was about thirteen, I started staying at home on my own rather than go to Josie's, but I always kept the phone by my side with Josie's number on speed dial.

Every moment that Dena wasn't at the office, she spent either working from home, at beauty parlours, or at social events that suited her needs. When I did not want to go with her for a full day of people touching me and putting creams and smelly stuff on my face, she would throw a tantrum and accuse me of never wanting to spend quality time with her. It was no use accusing her in return or reminding her of the many, many hours I had spent alone in the house, or of the important events that she had just not bothered to show up for in my life. No, I quickly learned that the best way to handle her outbursts was to leave the house. Most times I would go to Josie's to escape my mother's wrath.

Our relationship was a volatile one, and we were never close or loving towards each other. It was merely one in which we went through the motions; Dena was always terribly concerned about what others thought. Since I could remember, I would endlessly dream of one day being as far away from her as possible, happy and with a family of my own – the complete opposite of what I had known all my life.

Arriving home from the airport, Josie, who had become our maid in later years, was there to greet us. She was my surrogate mother, my confidant, and she greeted me with a curious smile that I knew translated into, 'How is her mood, must I tread on eggshells or not?'

I smirked, and Josie knew I meant, 'Yep, stay away.'

I had never wanted for anything materialistic in my life. I went to the best schools money could buy and always had the most fashionable wardrobe in comparison to all my snobbish school acquaintances. Of all the designer outfits hanging in my closet, I preferred jeans and T-shirts. I was the first in my class to get a car, and it hadn't just been any car, it was a Mercedes-Benz. Yet, I had never been an overly happy child. I would spend every free moment I had in my room or with Josie and her daughter, Patty, who had always been a real friend to me, more like a sister.

After giving Josie a hug, I immediately retreated to my room and to my books once again to finish my assignment, submission due date was in two days' time.

After graduating from school, everyone, especially Dena, had assumed I would go to the best and greatest university and get a degree in something Dena wanted me to study. I'd have the application forms shoved in my face on many occasions along with a string of threats and tantrums. I did not budge. I found myself being stronger than Josie, Patty or I had ever imagined I could be in resisting Dena. I got my way on the condition that I went to work for a company she recommended and that I studied investment banking part-time.

I did both for a year, and then resigned and started with an Events Management Diploma. I cannot explain or describe the scene that took place that night. I only really remember that it would have made an award-winning scene from a movie and that I had walked out and gone to a hotel for a few nights until she calmed down.

My room wasn't just a room but a cottage on the side of the house. It had a quaint feel to it with a thatched roof, wooden floors and large sliding doors in every room rather than windows. The lounge, kitchen and dining room were open-plan. There were two bedrooms; mine an en suite and the other had a guest bathroom between the two bedrooms. I used the spare room as a study since I never had guests.

I had wanted to move into a place of my own when I started working at Luxous, a furniture manufacturing company in Somerset West. But, when Dena suggested renovating the house for me I was touched as this was very out of character for her. I could come and go without ever having to enter the main house, which suited us both.

Josie lived with her husband Marco, and Patty, in a small house in the Strand area. Josie, I'm convinced, could have found employment elsewhere and had a better employer by far, but she loved me like a daughter, and I would be forever grateful to her for sticking with us – without her who knows how I would've turned out.

Chapter Two.

Patty and I made our way through the crowds and crowds of people mingling about at the annual car show. This show always took place at the Aerodrome in the Cape Town city centre.

Patty loved cars, bikes, planes and anything that had an engine. Josie constantly joked that she should have been born a boy. She always preferred to be with her father, Marco, either at his workshop or home working on their car in the garage with him.

Once she finished school, Patty went to work with Marco at his workshop, where, besides doing the usual car repairs, they also renovated vintage cars.

She was a tomboy but an elegant one at that. Josie had fought hard and well to nurture a little princess in Patty throughout her early youth but to no avail. Perhaps this was why Josie had always been so fond of me – I did all the girly things with her that uninterested Patty.

Patty was almost as tall as I was, with dark hair and eyes that her Spanish genes provided through her father.

Dena's famous words to Josie on many occasions were, 'Why doesn't that daughter of yours do something with her appearance? She could pass as a lady instead of a common girl.'

It would infuriate me, but Josie always said, 'Take it from whence it comes and just ignore her.'

Marco and Patty had both been slightly jealous, even if they'd never said as much, of the Mercedes Benz I'd received from Dena when I'd turned sixteen. But I'd hardly ever driven it – Patty always had the honour of driving it every morning when she dropped me at my school on the way to hers, and when she picked me up in the afternoon on her way home.

As soon as I was able to, I'd sold it and bought myself a small Golf convertible. Marco, Patty and my mother were horrified; Josie gave me a high five.

As we walked through the show, Patty gave me a detailed description of every car we passed or stopped to look at, even those that I never even knew existed. I merely listened without putting anything she said to memory. Naturally Patty knew a lot of the people at the auto shows, having been to most of them, so, in between stopping to look at the cars, we stopped to chat with several people. I tagged along beside her, trying to look as inconspicuous as possible. Often I would be asked for my opinion and every time I would see Patty freeze, fearing how I might reply. It gave me great pleasure to tease Patty because she knew this would happen and she knew I would answer with a load of rubbish. Sometimes she would cut in before I had a chance to reply and inform the poor person that I did in fact not know anything and that I was only there because I was her best friend. On the odd occasion, though, I made her pay for dragging me around for hours among cars, cars and more cars and all their spare parts.

'What do you think of the new V8 compared to the last model?' the young enthusiast had asked me.

'Well, it's certainly a different colour, this time, and I'm pretty sure the last one also had four wheels so then I guess there is not much difference,' I had replied smiling at Patty.

'Don't take any notice of her! Vanda, stop it please!' Patty had hastily taken my arm and dragged me along to the next car.

I did enjoy going with her; we always had fun wherever we went. As we finally sat down to have something to eat at the tables in the middle of the food court, I noticed that some of the lads Patty had been talking to earlier were approaching our table, and I told Patty as much.

'Oh please Vanda, don't speak about anything car related please, please?'

I smiled at her; it was always such a pleasure to see her beg me to keep quiet. She never knew if I would keep my word or not. They joined us and spoke to Patty about the cars and the show. I looked around and amused myself watching the different shapes and forms of so many different people passing our table. Whenever anyone asked me a question, I shoved a bite of my burger into my mouth so that I had an excuse not to answer. On any other subject, though, I spoke without hesitation.

I noticed that Patty seemed particularly interested in talking to a certain lad called Liam. When I excused myself to go to the ladies' room, Patty remained keenly in conversation with Liam. For the rest of the car show, we wandered around as a group. It was surprisingly pleasant, even though I was the only one not learned in the automotive world. The people I had just met were well-mannered and full of laughs. Not what I had expected at all.

As Josie always told me, 'Do not judge a book by its cover, beneath the dusty covers lies a body of feelings.'

I would always reply, 'That means Dena's book is the shortest story in the world,' and she would giggle and tell me not to be nasty.

Somehow amid all the chaos and other people, Marco and Josie managed to find us, and, after a quick introduction, Marco was talking and comparing notes with the young enthusiasts, and they were in awe of his knowledge, hanging onto his every word.

Josie and I grabbed the opportunity to escape and get some ice-cream and talk about anything, not car related. After buying our ice-creams, we linked our free arms and wandered, without any direction, between the cars and groups of people.

I stiffened for a second and gripped Josie's arm tightly, dragging her in another direction. Josie, not at all expecting such a sudden motion, stumbled as she tried to firstly, figure out what had happened and secondly, to correct her footing.

'What are you doing?' she scolded me.

'I'm so sorry, I just saw one of my bosses, the nasty one, and I most definitely do not want to be anywhere near him.'

We picked up our pace, still with our arms linked, and found our way back to our group.

The rest of the day we spent among the cars and people, and I nervously watched out for Trey. I found him to be a despicable person; rude, arrogant and with no regard for anyone but himself.

Alongside the car show and starting at eight o'clock that evening, our favourite local band was performing. As the time drew closer, we excitedly made our way there after saying goodbye to Marco and Josie who did not share our enthusiasm for loud music and screaming fans – they elected to go to a restaurant for some quality time alone.

Patty and Liam could not be separated; I had never seen Patty so eager to remain in a male's company since I'd known her. Liam was the same height as Patty, with ginger hair and deep green eyes. He had sharp but kind features, a soft voice and a seemingly gentle nature.

The band struck the first few beats, and the frenzy began. We danced, we jumped, we screamed at the band, we screamed at each other – sometimes just for the fun of it and sometimes to try and say something above the noise. With our new group of friends we were ten and here on common ground it felt as though we'd known one another forever.

After the show and several encores, we were not ready for the night to be over, and so off we headed to a restaurant-type bar that always stayed open until about three o'clock in the morning. Naturally Patty and Liam sat together while I sat opposite them, enjoying the rest of the conversation, even enduring the occasional car chatter.

Finally, Liam said he had to go otherwise he would not get up in time, and the rest of the group agreed with him.

'What have you got to get up for it's Sunday tomorrow?' I asked, curiously.

Liam looked at me in surprise as he answered, 'For church!'

Chapter Three

Thursday was the day we had our meetings. An odd day to have them, but since the boss, Mr Drake wanted them on this day we did not dare argue. Though on many occasions, the sales staff pleaded to have the meetings moved to another day as they needed to see clients on Thursdays. We all requested Mr Drake to change the weekly meeting to a Friday, but this interfered with his personal life and was therefore not approved.

Trey was his usual awful self, yelling and demoralising the sales staff; he seemed to think that because Mr Drake was such an awful boss, he should emulate him or be worse. I had seen grown men get up and walk out of the meeting, crying, never to return because of Trey. I, for one, could not see myself working here for much longer, it was no wonder there was such a huge turnaround of staff.

After an hour of our bosses complaining at everyone's performances and the lack of achieved targets, we left the meeting to go back to our respective offices.

It's almost your last year, just get your diploma then you can leave, stick it out Vanda, I kept telling myself.

The urge to hand in my resignation was so overpowering at times that it took an immense amount of self-control and willpower, and also a lot of convincing from Josie, for me to stay. Fortunately, I was just a junior employee and therefore not in the monster bosses' firing line, and so I managed to hold out.

I got home, threw my bag on the chair in my room and was busy taking off my shoes when I heard Dena knock on my door and enter without waiting for me to respond, as was our habit. I was usually a bit more cautious entering her house than she was mine because I was never sure whether she would be alone or entertaining a male "friend".

'I have an event you can do for your diploma on the tenth of March. One of the junior bankers is having a surprise party for her parents' fortieth wedding anniversary, and when I told her that you're studying event management, she agreed to speak with you.' Dena sounded impressed with herself and at the same time, I heard, 'You can't do this without me,' in her voice.

'Thanks, Mom, I appreciate it, I'll call her tomorrow.'

I was grateful for the opportunities I got via Dena's contacts. I knew very well I would not have been able to do the practical side of this course on my own, especially when it came to the quality of events I had been fortunate enough to organise. I showed my appreciation every time, even when the deal did not go through. But, when out of spitefulness she would tell other people that I could not do it without her, she truly got my blood boiling. It was an endless tug of war that existed between the two of us, a constant battle of malice and resentment.

She put the contact details on the kitchen counter and left. I picked up the note, and, reading the name while opening the fridge to look for something to eat; I felt excited. I did enjoy this line of work, and I knew the choice I had made to change my career had been the right one.

I phoned Patty to tell her, and she was as happy as I was. I was chatting with her and was about to sit down on my bed when suddenly I heard thunder roll and lightning strike so loudly that the glass doors of my cottage shook viciously. I got such a fright that I missed the bed, falling to the floor with a thud and rolling over onto my side with the momentum, my legs, arms and the phone sent sprawling in different directions. When I had untangled myself and found the phone, Patty was still on the other end calling my name. I burst out laughing, trying, between guffaws of laughter to explain to her what had happened. In Strand, a few kilometres away, Patty was experiencing the same wild weather as Somerset West, and she just laughed at me.

When we finally calmed down enough to have a decent chat, she told me that Liam had contacted her and that they were going out on an official date. She did not seem to be nervous but was more anxious as to whether she should get dressed up or not. They were going to the same restaurant we had gone to after the rock concert; she couldn't decide.

We spoke for at least an hour before hanging up. I was so happy for her, she was a stunning woman and deserved nothing less than a man that would treasure her. The fact that Liam was a petrol-head and already introduced to Marco made him even more of a perfect candidate. I couldn't wait to visit their home the next day, well aware of how Marco, Josie and I would tease Patty to bits. She wouldn't mind, though, we all loved a joke and often teased one another.

On my way to work in the morning, I phoned Marlette to arrange a meeting, with only a month and a half until her parents' anniversary, she was eager to meet me that same day, and hurriedly I agreed to meet during lunch.

Marlette was punctual and very much to the point. I could see why she was in banking. She never smiled, wanted to discuss business and leave; that she did after a single cup of coffee and twenty minutes of my time.

'She positively works with my mother,' I snickered to myself.

Josie and I sat on Patty's bed while she got ready for her date with Liam. We tried very hard to make her nervous but the more we tried, the more relaxed she became. Not exactly the reaction we were hoping for and not exactly a normal reaction when anticipating a first date. But, Patty was special that way. She giggled, jumped up off the bed after finally putting on her shoes and announced that she was ready. She looked lovely; casual but elegant at the same time, wearing black pants with a blue long-sleeved shirt, a denim jacket and a scarf.

We made our way from the bedroom to the living room where Marco; comfortably nestled himself on the couch in front of the TV. Josie, tripping and skipping behind Patty, squealed like a little girl at Marco to look at their daughter ready to go on her date. Marco looked sideways, gave her a long stare and turned to the TV again as he casually said, 'Josie, lock the door, my baby girl stays a baby girl. No dating allowed.'

Patty sat next to her dad and cuddled up to him, 'Just think Daddy, there will be another man in the house, sort of evens things out here a bit, don't you think?'

She put her arm around him. I loved the affection that so spontaneously swung around the house. It was a home, and once you were in it, you never wanted to leave. It's not as if this was Patty's first date, we had both dated less than most but more than a few times, but this was the first time I had seen Patty so comfortable with someone. It was as though she knew this was it, the last of the enduring dates searching for the perfect partner. As for me, I was far from nearing the end, or so I thought.

Before long, there was a knock at the door. Patty wrestled herself from her father's arms and let Liam in, who was smartly dressed in jeans and a brown casual shirt. He greeted everyone politely and after a few pleasantries they left.

There was no way I was going home – I was, without a doubt, sleeping over so that I could get the low-down from Patty the minute she walked in the door; I didn't care what time it was.

Josie and I sat in the kitchen nook, and she helped me plan the anniversary event. Fortunately, I had been given a reasonable budget by Marlette. We went through my trusted checklist, googled venues and caterers and had our usual bag of laughs with coffee and popcorn. We enjoyed recording Marco's obscene snoring while fast asleep on the couch, with the intention of using the video as a weapon against him one day. By eleven o'clock Josie was exhausted and made her way to bed, dragging Marco with her. I made myself comfortable on the couch to await Patty's return.

I must have fallen asleep because suddenly I woke up to the sound of the front door opening. I could hear Patty whispering her goodbyes to Liam, and then the door clicked closed. I sat up like a bullet.

'So, tell me!' I urged without wasting a second.

Much to my amusement, Patty squealed as she took a few steps back. I giggled and had to cover my face with a cushion to stifle my laughter for fear of waking up Marco and Josie.

'Wow, you gave me such a fright!' she said as she flopped onto the couch next to me.

For the next two hours, I got a detailed, comprehensive, almost step-by-step re-enactment of how the evening had gone. She was glowing, completely, and utterly smitten, and I presumed so was Liam. As expected, they were meeting each other the next afternoon after lunch. Liam was first going to church and then to visit his parents before picking her up. She wasn't sure where they were going and was not exactly bothered as long as she was with him.

Chapter Four

During a normal boring day at the office, I got a message from Marlette; she had accepted my quote, and I was to go ahead with the planning of the event. I received the guest list via email a few seconds later and a copy of the deposit payment. I was ecstatic; my portfolio was building up nicely. In just over a year my exams would be over, and I would feel confident enough to leave this evil place and start my own business.

Immediately I took my lunch break and made my way to the staff room, or, as it was officially called - the relaxation room - connected my laptop and confirmed the venue, caterers and paid the deposits.

The next Saturday would be spent shopping for various décor items and visiting florists. On Sunday, I would be going out with Patty and Liam. Liam was now a daily visitor at the Perez house and Patty and Liam were quickly developing a strong relationship.

A pleasant change of scenery was Bikini Beach in Gordon's Bay. I was sure we would've spent the afternoon around cars of some sort. With what was now becoming a good circle of petrol-head friends, we enjoyed the baking sun and sea and sand.

We played with a Frisbee and set up the volleyball nets, made up teams and played until our bodies hurt from the constant unusual movements our muscles had to make. Not a very sporty person, I was not much help to my team. Although we won, in the end, it was no thanks to me. When I had to serve, the ball did not even make it over the net. When the ball came my way, and there was no option other than to hit it, the ball would go plonking to the side and out of bounds, or it would land on the head of the poor person in front of me. Needless to say, the opposing team targeted me, knowing they would score points off my lack of coordination. I was concerned, at first, that being competitive lads they would get annoyed at my messing up so much, but instead, they found it extremely funny, making jokes at my expense throughout the day. One of the lads, Egan, who received several shots from me to the head, decided it was time to play touch rugby. Patty and I sat this game out. Who knew where the ball would land up if we played? We made ourselves comfortable on our towels and admired a bunch of surfers riding the waves in a determined fashion. We watched the lads with their endless energy run up and down after whoever had the ball, and chatted aimlessly, soaking up the sun.

Our conversation moved towards my upcoming event and the successful shopping day I'd had the previous day. The only thing left for me to do now was arrange the seating and the name cards for the tables. Patty changed the subject to Liam at every chance; they were more in love with each other as every second. I could not imagine a more perfect match for two people than Patty and Liam.

My eyes kept flickering to Egan. He was not much taller than I was, with thick brown wavy hair and grey eyes and a few freckles sprayed over his nose. Although he had been in the country for two years already, his Irish accent was still very strong. If he got annoyed at having to repeat himself continuously so we could, in fact, understand what he was saying, he never showed it.

I had to tell Patty about this strange attraction I was feeling towards him. We giggled and continued to watch the lads play their touch rugby, and the surfers beat one wave after another. Patty promised, under threat, of course, not to say anything to Liam. A feeling of nostalgia washed over both of us as we reminisced about being little girls back at school sharing stories about our boy crushes.

They finished their game and came running towards us a little too fast for my liking. Before I could voice my concern, Patty and I were whipped up, our objections unheard as we screamed and squealed. The sea was upon us within seconds, and we got flung into the oncoming waves like sacks of potatoes.

As we went under the water, the waves broke over us, pounding us and tossing our limp unsuspecting bodies around like rubber dolls in the wind. We clambered and fought our way to what we suspected was the surface. We gasped for the air our lungs were bursting for, and we wiped the water from our eyes and the hair from our faces. Then we swam hastily back to land, kicking with as much strength as we could muster.

At the shoreline we staggered and swayed and splashed our way onto the sand, trying to get as far away from the sea as possible and into a hysterical crowd of lads. Patty landed Liam such a punch on the arm that he probably felt it all of the next week. Jude offered us towels to dry off as we made our way back to our spot on the beach, where we had to endure the various angles and scenarios of how we had looked during our little dunking escapade.

Not wanting to leave the perfect weather and company, we sat relaxing under the umbrellas, learning more about our newfound friends and waiting in anticipation for the sun to set. I felt my skin tingling from too much sun. I couldn't remember when the last time was that I had been in the sun for so long in one day. As I applied moisturiser to my skin, I could feel the salt and sand that had stuck to it. I felt grubby and thought eagerly of the cleansing shower that awaited me. The state of my skin, however, did not detract from the beautiful sunset that was now on display, and with the last breath of the sun for the day, we raised our cups and said cheers.

Reluctantly we started to pack up our things, even David and Nathan's girlfriend's Katrin and Tania respectively were not keen on leaving. Having met them for the first time today, we got on like a house on fire. They kindly informed us that our dunking escapade had happened to them too; it seemed to be a form of initiation by the young lads. One day we would have our revenge the four of us agreed.

We made our way back to the cars with arms full of empty cooler boxes, chairs, towels and umbrellas – how did we get it all to the beach in the first place? My skin was tingling even more, and I was stickier than before. I could hear my shower calling me, but I didn't want to say goodbye just yet so I invited everyone to my cottage for coffee. The cleansing shower would just have to wait.

While I was making coffee and everyone was lounging comfortably under the lapa, Egan came into the kitchen and offered to help. As he stood against the fridge, he noticed my guitar leaning against the back of a chair and immediately went to pick it up and strummed a few cords. He could play! I was most impressed.

'Do you play?' he asked in his broad Irish accent.

'Yes,' I replied, 'but don't ask me to sing, I just can't!'

We both laughed and argued that my singing could not be worse than his while he made himself comfortable and started to play bits of songs, until I was ready to take the coffee out to everyone.

Under the lapa, we enjoyed our coffee, told stories of our lives, although I did not venture to tell any, and we listened to Egan play my guitar while the others sang along. Patty and I listened to the beautiful harmonies sung with such passion, both wishing we knew the words so we could join in. Katrin told us they were songs they always sang at church when they got together for their young adult meetings. They were soothing and inviting, and I wanted to learn them all.

My heart sank to my toes as I heard Dena's car pull into the garage and, as expected, she made her grand entrance greeting me with false affection so as to impress the others. She sat for a while and listened to the singing, but when she realised they were songs from church, she found an excuse to leave. Patty and I breathed sighs of relief. Everyone seemed a little curious with my relationship with Dena, and I gave Liam permission to fill them all in on the way home. Patty, Marco, Josie and I had told him my entire life story one night over dinner at the Perez's.

Someone mentioned a specific type of car, and that's when the singing stopped, and they all turned back into petrol-heads. Not knowing what on earth they were talking about, I took my guitar from Egan and sat quietly in the background strumming out some songs I knew.

At last, I was in the shower, relishing the cleansing, refreshing feeling over my body. I began to feel renewed, the tingling from the sunburn subsiding as the water washed over me. I stood smiling as I reminded myself that Egan had asked permission to come and visit and promised to bring his guitar along so he could teach me all his lovely church songs. It had been such a perfect day, and I had enjoyed it so much. My mind was so far away, and I was not paying much attention to what I was doing, so much so that I turned the cold water off first and the sudden intense heat burned my already sensitive skin. I yelled and jumped sideways into the wall, bashing my funny bone, which was just not funny at all.

Finally, I made it out of the shower safely, and I drowned my body in moisturiser with the hope that my skin would not peel. When I saw my face in the mirror, I burst out laughing at how hideous I looked. My face was bright red except around my eyes where my sunglasses had been. With my normally pale complexion, I looked ridiculous.

Chapter Five

It was easy to tell from her phone message that Patty was very excited. Liam asked her to go with him to church on Sunday. She wanted me to go along and of course, I agreed. I was interested to see what it was that made these people so happy, so genuine and so kind. They were certainly different; as if they weren't afraid of anything bad happening to them.

At home in my cottage that evening I pondered on whether or not I should tell Dena about going to church. She had never shown any interest in going to church or had ever even been in the slightest bit curious about religion. As a child, I had asked the usual questions a child with a developing mind asks. Questions like, 'Where do we come from?' 'Who created the earth?' 'What happens when we die?'

To all of them I got the same answer, 'What does it matter? We are here and when we die we won't see anyone on earth anymore.'

I got more answers to satisfy my curious mind from Josie and Marco. I had always had a longing and a desire to know more about the things called "church" and "religion" and was secretly hoping to find all my longed for answers on Sunday.

I decided to tell her and ask if she would like to join us, her reaction was no more surprising than I had expected.

'Don't be pathetic, as if that would interest me. I can't imagine why you would want to go there!'

Her reply hurt me even though I had no idea why, it was best for me just to turn away and go to my cottage. It was no use talking to her when she was in that frame of mind, and I was clearly disturbing her.

Back in the cottage, I cuddled up to the cushion on the chair in front of the TV. It was difficult to get Dena's comments out of my head; I wish I could understand why she was so against going to church. She had always made it very clear that she did not need anyone in her life; that she had made her fortune all on her own without anyone's help.

'No one will help you get rich, only you,' she would often tell me.

That was not what was important to me. I knew there had to be something else, something more. This could be the reason we clashed most of the time; our priorities were so vastly different. I was not watching what was on the TV and fell asleep still cuddling the cushion. I must've fallen into such a deep sleep as I did not even hear my phone ringing and woke up after about two hours of being curled up in an armchair. My skin was tingling again from the sunburn; I needed to put more cream on before climbing into bed. As I stood up from the chair, I realised too late that my legs had gone to sleep, and they failed to take my body weight, sending me falling over the coffee table landing halfway over the other chair. Was I awake now? I think so!

Recovering, I found my phone jammed down the side of the armchair, checked it for messages and found a message and a missed call from Egan. Now I was awake and very happy, and my heart started racing as I read his message. He wanted to come and visit me the following night, would I mind or was it too soon.

Would I mind? Eagerly I sent a reply, first apologising for not answering his call and then to confirm that he was more than welcome and that he must not forget to bring his guitar along.

When I got up in the morning and checked my phone, there was a message from Egan confirming that he would be at my house at seven o'clock. Immediately I agreed to myself that this was a great way to start the day, and I enthusiastically messaged Patty; her reply was as excited as my message.

On my way to work, I kept scratching my shoulders, wondering why they were itchy. I did not ponder on my shoulders very long as I found myself wondering about Egan's forthcoming visit that evening and I became rather nervous just thinking about it. I did like him, he was unlike most men I had met and dated, granted I did not know him very well and had not yet gone on a date with him. But I could just tell that he and his group of friends were different from most people and very likeable.

A day like any other at the office, I sat at my desk wishing the time would pass swiftly. I couldn't wait for seven o'clock; it was all I thought about. I honestly could not concentrate on my work; it was boring and irrelevant. All I wanted to do was be at home. Marlette sent me an email requesting an urgent meeting at lunch and apologising for inconveniencing me at such short notice. I did not mind the distraction; it would help me get through the hours until seven o'clock. I wondered if she was going to cancel the event that was in eleven days' time, but I found it difficult to even concern myself. I could not stop thinking about Egan.

I waited for ten minutes before Marlette arrived, immediately ordering herself a cup of coffee. Her concern was that there were another two couples on the guest list and whether this would be a problem for me.

Really, this was her big concern?

I took her piece of paper with the new guests' names on and assured her emphatically that it would be absolutely no problem whatsoever. She finished her coffee and left.

Still the same Marlette.

I still had half an hour before I had to be back at the office and I used the time to buy some snacks and a cool drink. Tonight! The butterflies flitted all over the pit of my stomach just thinking about it. I just had to tell someone. I phoned Patty, who threatened to spoil my evening by coming to visit. I nearly exploded, threatening her with all sorts of vicious acts, laughing at the same time which made her take my threats even less seriously.

'Okay, so I have to tell you what Liam said on Sunday night,' Patty was winding my excitement up another level.

'Egan couldn't stop asking Liam about you all the way home after they had dropped me off. He told Liam that he hadn't felt this way for a very long time.'

She remained silent waiting for my response, but I took a while before I replied, savouring every word she'd said. I was feeling very much like a little school girl, as the butterflies escalated along with the nerves and excitement.

Finally, I could leave the office; the day just would not end, dragging my nerves to the very ends of their tethers. Rushing home I had a shower and changed into a comfortable pair of jeans and a T-shirt, as fast as was humanly possible. Ensuring the cottage was neat; I sat on the couch in front of the TV for a few minutes, then got up and pottered around in the kitchen wishing for seven o'clock to come.

Dena walked in and looked at me curiously, 'And now, what's up? You look like a chicken on egg shells.'

'Egan is coming to visit. I like him a lot.'

'Is he one of the boys that were here on Sunday evening?'

'Yes.'

'Oh, please Vanda, they're such goody-two-shoes churchy people, honestly what do you see in them?'

'Mother, please just leave. I happen to like them.'

I could feel my blood pressure starting to rise rapidly. She turned on her heels and slammed the door shut behind her. She infuriated me and caused my nerves to bounce all over the place, from anger over her maliciousness to the anticipation of Egan's arrival.

Then the doorbell rang. My nerves ran out of my skin at a hundred miles an hour. I paused before going to the door, taking a long deep breath.

'Calm down, calm down,' I whispered to myself over and over. It didn't help. I rushed to the door fiddling with the door handle until it eventually opened. Egan stood in front of me with a smile as big as the doorway. He held a single white lily in one hand and his guitar and a packet of something in his other. I smiled back quite sure my lips were trembling and held tightly onto the door to steady myself.

'Hello, you ready to learn some songs?' he smiled, his Irish accent still so thick.

I wasn't sure what he'd said so I stepped aside as he entered the cottage.

'Please make yourself at home,' I spluttered.

Egan put his guitar down on the chair and emptied the contents of the packet onto the kitchen counter. I put the cool drink he'd brought into the fridge and the crisps in a bowl, dropped half of the crisps onto the counter top, and cleaned them up afterwards, embarrassed.

We sat on the couch together, jittery, and talking about our days since we'd last seen each other on Sunday. We both couldn't stop smiling, knowing that both of us were so very nervous.

'So where is your guitar?' he asked, picking up his and taking it out of its case.

I had forgotten to bring mine into the lounge and I hurried to fetch it. When I returned to the lounge, I rested it on the chair and first poured us another drink. Placing the glasses on the table, I sat on the couch and picked up my guitar, ready for my lesson.

While we sat holding our guitars ready to play, Egan told me how they would sit around fires at youth camps or even in the classrooms at the church building after their Bible studies and sing songs. How eagerly they loved to learn and to make up new ones. He handed me song sheets-he'd copied of all the songs and while I looked over them he played and played beautifully. After I'd listened to a few songs I attempted to play with him. It was a bit tricky at first but the more we played, the more in tune with the song and each others' strumming we became. I loved it. Never in my life had I played so well and so comfortably with someone else. The songs were lifting up my soul and my heart even though I did not understand them.

After a couple of hours of blissful music-making, we put our guitars to rest. I told Egan over and over how much I had enjoyed the evening, how much I had fallen in love with the songs and how much I appreciated that he'd taken the time to teach me.

Unconsciously I started scratching my upper arms, the moisturiser starting to wear off and the dryness of my skin from the excess sun beginning to irritate me again.

'So, you're coming to church on Sunday?' he smiled.

'Yes, I have no idea what to expect, though, as I've never been to church in my life.'

'Don't expect anything, just come along with an open heart; you might be surprised at what you find.'

'Pardon?'

'Don't expect anything, just come along with an open heart; you might be surprised at what you find,' he repeated himself slowly and deliberately.

In his thick Irish accent he told me about himself, repeating himself several times, in between gobbling snacks and pizza, playing on his guitar and my scratching. He told me he'd come to South Africa two years ago on a three-year contract for the Irish Embassy in South Africa. They gave him a loan to get his degree on condition that he worked it back over six years. He met Liam at a work function and Liam introduced him to the group of friends and also to God and His Church. He'd grown up in the coastal town of Wicklow, south of Dublin where his younger sister and his parents had resided all their lives. Coming to South Africa was his first venture outside of The United Kingdom, and it surprised me that he had not been to any other countries in Europe.

'Travelling was never in their setup,' he said matter-of-factly.

I crossed my legs on the couch, leaned comfortably back into the cushions, rubbed my back a few times across the cushion surface and scratched my arms some more. I told him about Dena, my lack of a father figure, and I told him about Josie, Marco and Patty, and how they made my life happy. Egan listened curiously and fed himself more snacks until I raised my arms and then rested them on the cushion with a thud.

'And that's my life story thus far,' I exclaimed, letting out a sigh as if relieved he hadn't run away yet.

'Glad you said "thus far",' he replied smiling a somewhat cheeky smile sending my heart racing out of my ears.

'You're scratching nicely, bet you start peeling by Friday,' he chuckled as I blushed, realising that I had been scratching increasingly as the evening had gone on, but, had became completely engrossed in Egan that I hadn't noticed. Excusing myself, I went quickly to my bedroom to rub more moisturiser on my itchy skin.

We flirted with each other continuously, with uncontrollable smiles and sparkling eyes until we realised it was one o'clock in the morning. Egan finally left, with his guitar under his arm and a lasting impression on my heart and my cheek from the soft, light kiss he placed there when saying goodbye.

Chapter Six

Marco and Josie were happy to see Patty and me getting ready to go to church, giving us encouragement and instructions as we got ready. We had no idea what to expect or how to dress, even though Liam and Egan had told us to dress casually. That could have several different meanings for a woman's wardrobe. I finally settled on a blue summer dress and Patty on a green skirt with a white gypsy top.

We arrived a little late; the church was already full of people sitting in the pews chatting to those next to them or reading the same news notice we had received on entering the building.

The church was charming and stylish, not enormous and lavish as I had imagined it to be and it felt very welcoming. I'm sure at a squash it could take at least three hundred people. There were three rows of pews leading up to the stairs that spread across the front of the stage. There was a board to left on the wall with six sets of numbers on it, and I immediately wondered why they were there. The people dressed very casually; in fact, Patty and I were overdressed, but they were exceptionally friendly. Little babies nestled in their parents' arms while toddlers and older children were moving around all over the show, making it look more like a crèche than a church. When a gentleman called out from the podium, everyone went quiet, and the children quickly made their ways to where their parents sat.

Even though we saw where Liam and Egan were sitting, we found an empty back pew and sat down; picking up the song books that had been resting on the pew waiting for us. We looked at each other and smiled nervously, looking around at all the people that seemed to be so enormously happy.

The gentleman at the front introduced himself as Garth and welcomed everyone to the worship service. He mentioned a few announcements that were relevant we presumed, to all the members rather than to us. To our surprise Tania's boyfriend, Nathan, stood up with the same song book we had and motioned everyone to stand; and we all duly did. He asked us all to turn to song number 302, and I realised this was what the numbers on the wall meant – I whispered as much to Patty, who nodded as we turned to song 302. Everyone began to sing with Nathan as did we though I should rather say we just mumbled along.

After the song we all sat down again and a man named Josh stood up at the podium. He told everyone he would be doing the Lord's Supper. It was all very interesting to us as we listened deeply to what he was saying, trying to understand the reasons for what they were doing. Pieces of communion bread and little cups of grape juice passed around from person to person, and once everyone had theirs, prayers were said, and everyone ate and drank then prayed silently. I felt so moved and determined to ask Egan to explain this to me in more detail. Nathan, requested everyone to stand up again and to sing another song. Two rows in front of us an old lady sneezed as she stood up and at the same time expelled what might classify as a squeaky fart. The people in the row in front of us snickered but continued to sing without any further ado. Patty and I looked at each other, with a combination of nervousness and anxiety, both of us had to cover our faces with our song books to hide our giggling. We couldn't stop as the giggling led to laughter that we had to try and stifle or else we'd cause a scene. The tears began to roll down our faces, and our shoulders started to shake as we laughed silently, still hiding our faces in our song books. The more we tried to stifle our laughter the more we wanted to burst out laughing. We had to leave the building.

Outside in the parking lot, we could finally burst out laughing and get the bubble of air out of our systems. Our laughter became so hysterical that our knees no longer allowed us to stand and we both sat down on the steps with a bump. It was not that the little old lady's fart had been unusually funny or unusual at all, but our nervousness had gotten the better of us, and the incident had been the perfect release.

It took a while for us to compose ourselves, to stop rethinking our stupidity enough to curb another outburst. I whispered to Patty that we go to the ladies bathroom to clean up our faces and to try and compose ourselves.

Finally, back on our seats, we rejoined the service about five minutes into Minister Wade's sermon. He had a voice that was captivating; one just had to listen to what he was saying. He spoke about Jesus and the eternal life He offered. He said one thing that stuck in my head for the rest of the day, actually for the rest of the week and then some.

He said, 'We will all die one day and so what? We will all leave this earth and leave our loved ones behind, and so what? The only thing that matters is where we go after we die. That is all that matters.'

Then he asked a question that also really stuck, 'Where are you going? Are you ready to die confidently? Do you know that when you die you can live forever? Are you ready?'

I sat still and silently for however long his sermon took – it could have taken the whole day, and I would have listened intently throughout; the episode with the little old lady long forgotten. The sermon reached into places in my soul that I had no idea existed.

Egan must explain this to me again someday soon; I pondered

After the service, Liam, Egan and the other friends we knew all met us outside the church building, and they dragged us back in again to have tea and coffee and to introduce us to the other church members. The question they were dying to ask was whether we had enjoyed the service, afraid that we might say no and never return. We put them at ease with our positive responses, and when we told them about our little old lady episode they found it hilarious and almost set Patty and me off again. Minister Wade rescued us by introducing himself. He naturally wanted to know a bit about who we were and how we knew Liam and Egan and whether we had enjoyed the service and, of course, he welcomed us back at any time.

Finally, Patty and I left with Liam and Egan in tow, and went to Patty's house, to two very eager parents waiting to hear all our news. They were undoubtedly extremely happy we had enjoyed it so much, and Liam invited them to join us next Sunday; Marco accepting the invitation before Liam had even finished asking. Josie had made a huge lunch and threatened us with our lives if we had other plans. If Liam and Egan did have, they very quickly cancelled for fear of Josie's wrath.

After an enormous lunch, we sat in their backyard beside the pool. It was a warm summer's day, but I was not going into the direct sun for anyone's sake. I was, as Egan had predicted, peeling all over my back and my upper arms and even on my face. I looked like a snake shedding its skin. It was as annoyingly itchy as it was hideous, and Patty found great pleasure in pulling the skin off my back like she was peeling an orange.

As expected, it was not long before the conversation turned to cars and other car related topics. Josie and I excused ourselves and went to the kitchen to clean up the dishes.

'They are such nice boys, I like them,' Josie said, nudging me in the side with her elbow.

'I know, it just seems so perfect sometimes that I worry it's too perfect.'

'It makes me and Marco so happy that you and Patty have found good-mannered God-fearing boys.'

'Now, now Josie, don't get ahead of yourself. Egan and I have not even kissed yet, and you're marrying us off already!'

'Oh you and Egan, and Patty and Liam, you're going to get married. I just know it.'

She said it so matter of fact she convinced me of its truth. A truth I wouldn't mind having come true.

We returned to the rest of them to find out that we were all going to the race track at Killarney Gardens the weekend after next to watch the racing.

'Oh yay, we get to see more cars and this time, they will be making loud noises. Maybe Josie, if we go back to the kitchen and come out again they will have changed their minds again, and we won't be going anymore.'

Josie snickered, but Egan seemed to think I was serious.

'I'm sorry, I wouldn't want you to go anywhere you don't want to go, sorry for making plans without asking you first,' he said, looking worriedly at me.

Egan's Irish accent wasn't so strong anymore, or rather perhaps I became more familiar with his accent.

I knew I had fallen in love with Egan; my heart was a complete mess of mush, listening to him sounding so concerned. Josie smiled at me while I'm sure she was seeing wedding bells in my eyes at the same time.

'It's okay, I'm only joking, it will be fine. Besides, Josie will keep me company when I get lost in translation,' I replied, laughing and instinctively placing my hand on his upper arm in reassurance.

'Excellent,' he happily said as he rejoined Marco and the other petrol-heads to talk about more cars I guessed.

The conversation switched back and forth from cars to church and back again, and in between, everyone except me took dips in the pool. We had a wonderfully relaxing day and the time went by as fast as it usually does when we enjoy a good time. And before we knew it, it was time for me to make my way home. Liam and Egan insisted they drive behind me to make sure I got home safely before making their way home.

I was hardly in the cottage when Dena was at my side asking questions. The more I emphasised how much I had enjoyed church and Egan's company, the more annoyed she became. The more annoyed she got, the more she insulted me, the church and Egan, until eventually I got angry and told her to get out.

Why did she always have to push it so far? I could just not understand why we would always end up having an argument; why she always had to resort to insulting everyone – my newfound friends were no threat to her whatsoever. I just didn't understand her.

As she left, slamming the door behind her, my phone buzzed.

A text message from Egan: *'Thx 4 a gr8 day, may I take you out 4 dinner 2moro nite?'*

My anger lifted instantly, and the smile stretched across my face all the way to my ears.

'I wld luv to go out 4 dinner with you thx 4 asking me,' I texted him back.

I danced my way to my room clutching my phone to my chest.

His reply came: *'Awesome, will pick you up at 7 pm. Sleep well, God bless.'*

I could have floated if it were possible. Dena could think and act how she pleased; she had no idea, and I doubted she could ever know what it felt like to be so happy.

As I stood under the shower, rubbing my skin and trying to remove the flakes, I relived the day in my head, from Minister Wade's meaningful words to Egan's eyes, smile and touch and then back to Minister Wade's sermon. I would talk to Egan on our date about what Minister Wade had said. I just had to find out more about what made this church so important to them.

Chapter Seven

I arrived home and was dying to get ready for my date with Egan; it was all I had thought about since his text message the previous night. In the driveway stood a car I did not recognise and after putting my bag down I went to Dena's house.

Probably another boyfriend! I thought and of course, I was right.

Where did she find these poor suckers?

Dena introduced me to Juan, a man, at least, ten to fifteen years younger than she, but I would wager that he did not know this. He was an acquaintance through work, and they were going on a date. I had to find out where they were going, as the last thing I wanted was to end up at the same restaurant with Egan. So whatever happened tonight, Egan and I would not be going to Tappa's. I made a polite exit and hurried to my cottage as soon as the door closed behind me.

As I showered and began to get dressed, my stomach rounded up all the butterflies it could, and they made their presence known. A smile appeared on my face, and every few minutes I would burst into a giggle. At last, I decided on a pair of black pants and a burnt orange hippie-styled shirt with leather sandals almost the same colour orange. I left my hair natural and loose and put on a smudge of make-up and a splash of perfume to finish me off; then I agreed that I was ready.

It was only six-thirty, and I had a full thirty minutes to wait before Egan arrived. Not a good thing for the relentless butterflies.

My cottage I kept clean and tidy on my own. I did not allow Josie to clean it; I had just too much respect for her aside from seeing her as my surrogate mother. However, I had to do something; just sitting, waiting, was only churning the butterflies into a frenzy. So, I got out the feather duster and dusted anything and everything. Finally, when the doorbell rang, I spun around and ran to the door, opening it in a matter of seconds. Egan faced me with a single white lily in his hand, and a huge smile, but he had a rather confused look on his face.

'Do we have to clean up before we leave?' he asked, looking at the brightly coloured feather duster in my hand.

I felt my face go red, and I laughed as I explained that I had needed to keep myself busy and moved aside to allow him inside the cottage. He gave me enough time to put the feather duster down and collect my jacket and bag before he ushered me out of the house and to his car. He held the passenger door open for me as I got in, and then closed it gently before moving around to the driver's side and sliding in behind the steering wheel. As he started his car, which seemed to be a smaller version of a Jeep, he rubbed his hands together and let out a boyish Irish laugh.

'Vanda, I have to tell you, I'm so excited and nervous at the same time. I've been dying to ask you out since that day on the beach – thank you for accepting.'

He just looked at me; he did not stare, but he just looked at me for a few seconds then turned to concentrate on reversing the car out of the driveway.

All I could say was, 'I'm so happy you asked me.'

It was quiet for a few minutes while we calmed our initial excitement and then I remembered Dena.

'Where are we going if you don't mind me asking?'

'Oh, I thought we might go to the carnival that's here for the week and eat loads of junk food unless you would rather go to a restaurant of course?

The carnival sounded so perfect that I giggled with glee. It was exactly the first date I would have wanted.

'No, that sounds perfect! How did you know I would enjoy this?'

'Well,' he said blushing slightly, 'I cheated! I phoned Patty and asked her what you'd prefer, the carnival or a fancy restaurant? She recommended the carnival. Do you mind that I phoned her?'

'Um, no, not at all; I think I must have a little word with my best friend tomorrow, though.'

'I hope I have not caused a problem?'

'No, silly, I'm just teasing you,' I patted his leg in reassurance.

The carnival site was brightly lit up with hundreds of lights; some flashing and all in a variety of colours. Walking towards the entrance, I could feel the carnival atmosphere pulling us towards it. Egan took my hand as we wobbled over the uneven grass that prickled my feet through my open sandals. My heart pounded, not from the walk but his touch, so much so that my concentration on steadily walking on the ground wavered just enough for me to put my foot into a small hole in the ground. If it were not for his strong grip around my hand, I would've met the ground unpleasantly and embarrassingly.

'Careful there, the ground is very uneven,' Egan said as if I did not know it.

He held me with both arms as I steadied myself and even though I was so very stupidly embarrassed, I thought I could have just stayed there like that with him holding me forever.

'You think?' I mumbled.

We finally got to the entrance safely, still holding hands. Egan paid the entrance fee refusing my offer to pay for myself, and we headed straight for the food stands, Egan holding me close to his side as if afraid I might get lost. I welcomed his gesture gladly.

'I'm starving. What do you feel like eating?' he said, already pulling money from his wallet.

I opted for a shwarma, and he chose to have a few boerewors rolls. Walking slowly to the makeshift eating area of tables and chairs, we found an open table and quickly sat down to enjoy our meal. I was so grateful for the chance to sit down and eat, as the shwarma became increasingly juicy and difficult to eat. I had to wipe my mouth with the provided serviettes after every bite, and if it were not for the table, half of my food would've been on my shirt. Egan was having similar problems with all five of his juicy boerewors rolls, causing us to laugh after every bite. Finally, we washed our food down with a can of cooldrink. We were full and satisfied and got up to walk around.

I noticed Egan looking at the high adrenalin rides and quickly told him, 'Please let all this food settle before we go on any of those rides unless you want my food returned for credit!'

He burst out laughing, 'I was thinking the same thing!'

With us both agreeing to wait before becoming adrenalin junkies, we amused ourselves with the stalls – shooting pellets at targets, throwing hoops over sticks, throwing balls at plastic bottles and laughing more than I had laughed all my life. We challenged each other at every turn, threatening to beat each other at every game. Sadly I lost them all, but it was amusing to see his macho male ego take over at the very thought of a woman beating him at anything.

By the time we made it to the big rides, our arms were so full of prizes, small teddy bears and silly toys, that Egan decided to put them in the car for fear of losing them on the rides. I patiently waited at the Big Wheel ticket office, hoping my food was at the base of my stomach by now and with no plans of returning. He joined me again after several minutes, panting and out of breath, so I guessed he had run there and back.

'Right, are you ready for this?' he asked, paying for our tickets and still refusing to let me contribute.

The Big Wheel did not offer the same rush of speed and sheer thrill that the Big Dipper would, but it gave us the opportunity to view the world in the dark, all lit up by sparkling lights. But most importantly it gave Egan the opportunity to put his arm around me without the chance of me running away. He took this chance, and I smiled, hugging his side. We sat grinning and watching the world go up and down as we rotated in huge circles.

'I've wanted to ask you if you would come over one night and explain to me a bit more what your minister preached about on Sunday, and also why you do that communion every Sunday?'

I spluttered, suddenly a little embarrassed.

'How about Liam, Patty and I come over tomorrow night, and we can talk about it? Apparently Patty was asking Liam the same thing.'

I agreed, and we sat in silence until the wheel came to a stop when we were at the bottom. From there we moved to the bumper cars, and that I even had a neck left afterwards was incredible. Egan pounded my car with his and so did everyone else that noticed what a useless driver and easy target I was.

Then we went to those crazy super fast swings that swayed out almost parallel to the ground as they went around and around and around. People were hooking their feet into the swings in front of them and pushing the person forward, so they spun as they went around. I begged the woman in the swing behind me not to do it to me, and fortunately, I was spared. I was flying parallel to the ground faster than I had ever moved in my life. When I looked at the ground I felt sick, if I looked up, I felt sick. The wind slapped my face. Once we were back on solid ground, we were so drunk from spinning so fast that we staggered around for some time before our brains fell into place again. I pleaded that we would not have to do that ever again.

After a few other exhilarating rides and lots of excitement, we finally reached the Big Dipper. Egan got into his seat and clamped down the safety bar. He rubbed his hands together, literally bubbling with excitement at the forthcoming adrenalin rush.

'I love this; it's such a rush.'

I did not care to answer him as the seats began to move. My heart disappeared to my toes as we climbed and climbed and climbed some more, hearing a clicking sound as the train of seats made its way to the top. I'd thought the Big Wheel was high. I let out a nervous cry as we finally reached the top, and warned Egan to close his ears. He did not care; he was laughing so much and bursting with eagerness to get this ride going. My heart made one solid movement from my toes to my head in a split-second as we dropped from zero speed to what felt to me like a thousand kilometres an hour. I screamed, but no sound came out, my eyeballs fell to somewhere at the back of my head, my hair reached for the stars and then I found my voice. There was no telling in which country my voice was heard, all I knew was that it was so loud it scared me. Egan laughed and laughed, thoroughly enjoying the rush. We were thrown from side to side, backwards and forwards and were shaken about as the train of seats sped around the bends and angles of the track.

When we came to a standstill, I couldn't get my hands to loosen the bar I was shaking so much. Egan remained in his seat, and I looked at him confused.

He smiled, 'I paid for two rides; we're going again.'

I wanted to pee my pants.

I had to go through this again, and the only thought that crossed my mind was that he was insane. The bars clicked shut again and away we went for another round of torture, Egan laughing and giggling in pure excitement. My adrenalin led me on a rollercoaster ride once again.

Finally, it ended, and the bars clicked open. I looked at Egan hesitantly in case he was going to horrify me with the words, 'We're going again.'

But he stood up as if he hadn't been on the ride at all and helped me to stand; it was difficult, my legs were like jelly, wobbling and shaking and my whole body was trembling, much to his amusement.

'You're nasty,' I scolded him as my body movements slowly normalised and the terror slowly eased from my bones.

'Sorry, I couldn't help myself! Please don't be mad at me, please,' he begged, as he put his arm around me hoping to appease any anger I might be feeling and also to help me walk.

How could I possibly be angry with him? I had just spent the best hours of my life with him, granted, it was not what I was used to, but he had his arm around me, and I would not jeopardise that for anything.

'I'm not mad, and even if it does not seem like it I am having fun,' I replied, reassuring him but not so much so that he would think I would want to go on that Big Dipper again.

We walked around for a bit longer then decided to leave, but first Egan had to have another two boerewors rolls, and we shared a drink. All the adrenaline had made him work up an appetite he explained, but I felt like I could never eat again.

We finally arrived at my cottage. It was already an early hour of the morning and Egan, as did I, thought it wise that he leave now rather than stay longer. I opened the cottage door expecting him to leave as agreed, but he walked in and shut the door behind him. I went to put my bag down on the kitchen counter, and it had barely touched the surface when Egan had his arms around my neck.

'May I kiss you? I've been dying to kiss you all evening,' he said, blushing and smiling at the same time as he moved his face so close to mine that I could feel his breath on my lips.

My nerves, the excitement, the adrenalin, the rides, the greasy food and the intensity of this moment all compounded just then as my food - that I convinced myself had settled at the base of my stomach - decided it hadn't and decided, after all, to return itself for credit.

'I'm sorry.' I gasped, as I pulled away and clutched my mouth, to prolong the inevitable just long enough to dash to the bathroom and get my head in the toilet. There was a split second before it was too late as the revolting flood of unsettled food made its way down the toilet.

I was so embarrassed I wanted to disappear down with the flushing water. I didn't think I would be able to go back to a stunned and bemused Egan still waiting patiently in the lounge.

'I'm so sorry. I am so sorry.' I apologised over and over again, once I had finally mustered up the courage to return to the lounge.

He just laughed and inquired as to whether I felt better, and then said he would see me the following evening for our study.

I was completely persuaded I would never see him again.

Chapter Eight

I had to wait until lunchtime before I heard from Egan. My heart was numb and heavy at the thought of what had happened the previous evening. I wanted to get sick all over again just thinking about it. It was horrifying.

I read his message slowly, not once, but several times *'Will pick u up 4 study 2nite. Hope u feeling beta xx'*

I insisted it wasn't necessary and that it would be out of his way since he lived closer to Patty than to me. He too insisted that we had some unfinished business we had to attend to, and if I wanted to be embarrassed, then I should insist on my way. After a second of deliberation and a few vivid images I relented.

I leaped out of my chair with a giggle and a squeak and did a little jiggle dance in absolute delight.

Dena walked into the cottage just as I was getting dressed.

'Where are you going?'

'I'm going to a Bible study at Patty's house. Egan is coming to fetch me in a few minutes. Do you want to come along?'

I knew that whatever her reply was it would annoy me, but I asked regardless.

'Oh my word, you have got to be kidding me, why bother with that nonsense? In any case, I am going out on a date again tonight.'

I was annoyed, and the spiteful side of me came pouncing out of the cracks.

'With your toyboy from last night? Is he not young enough to be your son? Does his mommy know? But more to the point, does he know how old you in fact are?'

'Just shut up Vanda, and no, it is a different man.'

'Jeepers, two young boys in two nights, you should rather be a vampire. At least, then you could have an excuse because this, what you are doing is just all kinds of wrong.'

She turned around and slammed the door on her way out, cursing me in words I had forgotten existed. I knew she would make me angry, and I knew I would retaliate as much as I did not want to, but I just could not control myself, I always let my anger get the better of me when it came to her, and that annoyed me even more.

Fortunately, enough time passed for me to calm down before Egan arrived. He gave a brisk tap on the door before I opened it. He was barely inside when his arms were around my waist, and he was pulling me to him, hugging me tightly as I clung on relishing the moment. I was sure time had stood still.

'Hello,' he whispered, smiling a huge sparkling Irish smile.

I didn't reply, there was no point, and I kissed him softly before either one of us could say or think anything else. My knees buckled, and I was never to love another. I knew so from the very instance our lips met.

'You're not going to get sick again are you?'

I flushed instantly

'I am so sorry about that. I was sure you would run away…'

He calmed my fears with a reassuring kiss before I could finish my sentence. We managed to tear ourselves apart to go to Bible study. I did not know a smile could stick to a face so effortlessly.

When we walked into the Perez house, our smiles and bright shiny eyes could not hide our feelings for each other, even if we'd tried. Naturally, Patty had received a phone call from me the first thing that morning, with a detailed report of our date and, of course, our attempted first kiss – it would be a moment I would never live down - so, of course, she had reported to Josie, Marco and Liam. I'm pretty sure Liam had heard all about it from Egan as well.

After much elation and many hugs, we were finally able to settle down around the dinner table with our coffee, study aids and Bibles in hand. Liam sat at the head of the table and began with a prayer as we all held hands. He asked Marco, Josie, Patty and me what we understood salvation to be and who we thought Jesus was. I felt incredibly stupid as I had no idea. Marco, Josie and Patty gave informed replies but since Dena had thwarted any remotely religious teachings or discussions when I was growing up, the only answers I had, I based on the good morals Josie had taught me.

Egan held my hand and patted it at the same time, as he smiled and encouraged me not to feel inadequate as that was why they were there, to help me understand; to teach us all the path to salvation. Liam continued with the study, and I listened intently as a new world was opened in front of me, beckoning me to know more. We all asked questions freely, most of the questions coming from me. However, Liam and Egan did not mind one bit and answered us every time with scriptures to substantiate their replies.

The evening flew by, but as we all had to work the following day, we needed to end the study session and agreed to meet on Thursday evening again. We agreed that to wait an entire week was too long.

On our way to my cottage, Egan told me how lonely he had felt in a strange country when he had first arrived in South Africa. Then he had met Liam and had been drawn by Liam's attitude towards life and people. He had an aura about him that was indestructible. When Egan had learned that it was God that inspired him, Egan had been fascinated as he, like me, had grown up in an environment without Christianity. His family was very stifled towards any church, claiming that the fighting between different denominations in Ireland had put them off any form of religion. When he had told them via a video call of his baptism, they had not been very impressed, but that only made him more determined to show them how life should be. I felt so much compassion for him, knowing what it felt like to have had no spiritual guidance at home whatsoever.

'So, you have your event this Saturday, what am I going to do with myself?'

'Well, you will have to do what you did before I came onto the scene.'

He laughed. 'No, that is just way too dull and boring. I will just have to irritate Liam and Patty for the day; just make sure you keep your phone on all day!'

'Well, I will need an extra pair of hands to set up the venue if you're interested?'

Before I could say anything else, he replied, 'Absolutely! I was hoping you would ask,' and he laughed happily.

As we pulled up into the driveway, we both noticed a strange car parked in front of Dena's garage door.

'Dena's having a friendly sleepover,' I said sarcastically, with a hint of distaste.

After making sure I was in the cottage safely, Egan said goodbye with a kiss designed to last forever.

Chapter Nine

The venue was open when we arrived to set up the décor. Egan's extra pair of hands helped tremendously, a fact that he playfully reminded me of throughout the day. The caterers arrived and got on with their business in the kitchen, fortunately not interfering with me and my extra set of hands. The tables and chairs neatly set out as I had requested, so we began by covering the tables with white table clothes and ruby-coloured overlays. In the middle of each table, we placed a glass vase a quarter full of water and then added a squirt of ruby-coloured dye. To each vase, we then added four ruby-coloured roses and a bit of greenery. Ruby organza tiebacks went around each white covered chair. Silver name tags with the names written in a ruby colour stood placed on top of ruby-coloured serviettes. We placed a silver 40 in the centre of the serviette, adding to the fortieth anniversary theme, celebrated with rubies. At the entrance, we set up the stands with photos of the celebrating couple, photos of their life together, and also a table with a book in which everyone could write them a message.

The final few things to do involved arranging a trolley for the cake and cleaning up the mess. Then we had to rush home and get cleaned up and then rush back looking decent, in time for the DJ, Leo, to arrive to set up his things.

Egan was already back at my place before I was ready, smelling fresh and looking dashing in a pair of grey pants and a black shirt. I wore a black summer dress but still had to dry my hair.

While he waited in the lounge strumming on my guitar, Dena walked in. He stood up as he greeted her and she smiled and for once was pleasant enough without trying to flirt. From my bedroom, I could hear them chatting above the noise of my hairdryer, which I hurried along. When I had finished, I practically raced into the lounge, not wanting Dena to be alone with Egan for a second longer than necessary. I found her sitting in the armchair, dressed casually and looking very relaxed. Egan seemed quite content too. It was rather unnerving.

'Egan says the hall looks lovely. I hope you have taken some photos so I can have a look,' she said, sounding genuinely interested.

Not entirely convinced, though, and every second I waited for her to change back into the Dena I knew. But she didn't, and we had a pleasant half an hour before Egan, and I had to leave. She greeted Egan decently when we left and wished me luck. He questioned me about her attitude as it was not how he had remembered her from his first meeting, nor from what I had told him. I just said I was as confused as he was and if only she would always be so agreeable.

We arrived back at the hall to find Leo waiting to be allowed in. Naturally Egan got involved in helping him, the two of them talking music and gadgets. I made my way to the caterers to ensure all was in place and the cake ready for its grand entrance. I gasped at the sight of the masterpiece, a perfect replica of their original wedding cake, two tiers with a waterfall of red roses falling over both tiers on the one side. It was the first time I had used these caterers, and I had been anxious as to their performance, but they seemed to have outdone themselves.

Marlette arrived early to inspect the hall, the food and the cake, and, once satisfied, or, at least, I hoped that was the case, she made a few phone calls and shortly after that the guests started arriving. Egan and I hung around in the background watching the guests with interest. I noticed that no one seemed to be smiling or even look pleased to be at the party and mentioned so to Egan; he agreed with me as we continued with our observations.

When at last the honoured couple arrived, everyone stood up, and as they entered the hall, everyone yelled out, 'Surprise!'

The wife shone with happiness while the husband looked very surprised indeed. Marlette ushered her parents to their seats as everyone clapped and Leo played the song Marlette had requested. Still no one seemed overly happy, besides the mother. I worried they were not happy with the décor or the venue or something that I hadn't done to their specifications.

A moment before the speeches I caught Marlette alone and asked if everything was fine without telling her that everyone looked miserable.

'Oh yes,' she replied, 'it is perfect, just what we wanted. Thank you, Vanda, you outdid yourself.'

Really? Then why is no one smiling? I was confused.

Everyone turned their attention to Marlette's father when he took the microphone, said a few words and then began to sing an acapella song dedicated to his wife. He had a magnificent voice, and sang to her and only her, directly from his heart. She smiled and stared at him with her soul while a few tears trickled down her cheeks. You could not have heard a pin drop as everyone focused on this most touching moment. A tear trickled down the side of my face as I engrossed myself in seeing such tender and loving devotion between two people.

As he came to the end of the song he got down on one knee, reached his hand out to his wife and sang the last few notes, then said, 'I love you my darling wife.'

Applause filled the hall while a few whistles and hurrahs sounded out from the guests. I felt a hand on my face and looked at Egan wiping away the falling tears. I giggled, a little embarrassed as he kissed me gently where the tears had fallen. He was about to say something that I am sure I would've wanted to hear when we were interrupted by the Master of Ceremonies. The moment would have to wait as I gave the go-ahead for the cake to make its grand entrance.

The cake was brought out on a covered trolley accompanied by another round of applause. The celebrating couple immediately recognised the perfect replica of their wedding cake and applauded along with the rest of the guests.

With all the formalities finally done I thought the guests would start smiling and begin to enjoy themselves, sadly, this was not the case. The honoured couple, however, hung on to each other's every word and movement, not in the least bit concerned by all their miserable guests.

I felt cheated, having made up a room to look so beautiful and joyous, only to have a bunch of miserable guests partake of it. Marlette was, in my opinion, the leader of the miserable pack. Egan and I left before we became as miserable as the rest of them and it was still a few hours before we would have to start cleaning up; that is if the party would even last that long.

As it was still summer, the sunset was only at approximately nine-thirty, which still gave us plenty of time to walk barefoot along the shore and appreciate the beauty of the last moments of the day. After a lovely stroll on the beach, we finally sat down on a bench to watch the sunset. It was a spectacular sunset, even more so with him sharing it with me.

It had been a strange day, not what I had anticipated at all. Dena had been unusually pleasant which had made me happy, but then the guests had been unusually miserable which had disappointed me very much. But, with the sweet always comes the sour I surmised, as I dropped my ice-cream all over my black dress sending Egan into a fit of laughter.

Was every romantic moment today going to be ruined?

Chapter Ten

As we stood in the queue at the entrance to the racetrack, it was very entertaining to watch the excited petrol-heads eagerly anticipating the upcoming event. It was all they could think or talk about – which car was in good form, who was off the pace, this new technology, that new spare part. But most of all, who would win the raffle to get five laps with the World Champion and Number One Driver of the Year in his brand new machine.

As we entered the arena and made our way to our seats, we passed a world-renowned driver and got very close to a famous racing car several times. If Marco, Egan, Liam or Patty could just so much as touch either they would've landed up in a frenzy, so great was their sheer love for this sport. At one time a driver standing near his car gave them a smile as we very, very slowly walked passed they all nearly fainted; their heart rate became so erratic.

I lingered a bit, holding onto Josie's arm as the others continued to make their way through the people, cars and drivers in complete awe. Josie and I stopped and asked the driver that had smiled to sign four pages of the little notebook I always carried in my bag. He obliged graciously and even asked for their names so he could address each note personally. Josie and I had absolutely no idea who Jason Mitchell was and therefore rather than make conversation and make fools of ourselves, we just thanked him and hurried back to the others before they realised we were not with them. We giggled with joy at our tiny achievement, knowing full well the reaction we would get.

Finally, we reached our seats and made ourselves comfortable, looking down onto the track and the officials as they went about their business ensuring they had done everything in their power to provide a safe and entertaining day's racing.

When everyone had calmed down enough to pay attention to me, I stood up and handed each of them a folded piece of paper. I sat down again as four yelps leapt from each of them simultaneously as they jumped up, looked at one another's little pages and yelled once more. Then an array of questions and thanks ensued. The autograph of Jason Mitchell was none other than that of the Number One Driver of the Year.

Josie and I gave each other high fives while the others continued to show their pieces of paper to anyone in the seats around us who looked our way. Egan hugged me and kissed me and smiled and laughed with delight; he read the little piece of paper, again and again, he was just so over-excited. It was unbelievable that a little piece of paper with a signature on it could make these precious people so ecstatic. Josie and I could have asked for anything within a hundred mile radius, and I could consider it done, they were that thankful.

The day soon reached mid-morning and although I had a hat on, the sun baked down hot as an oven. I realised that the three-quarter cotton pants and sleeveless shirt I was wearing provided little or no protection from the blazing sun, and that no amount of sunscreen would prevent me from getting burned - this would entail another flaking and itching ordeal in the days to come. Egan, even in his complete intoxication of the racetrack and its fumes, noticed with concern that I was rubbing my arms.

'Did you not bring anything along to cover your arms? You'll get burnt to toast in this sun, trust me; I have scars from the blisters to prove it. I always bring extras, you never know who might forget to bring something,' he said, fussing in his backpack until he pulled out a light jacket, sporting a rather cheeky Irish grin.

'Vanda,' he said in a moment of seriousness, 'this autograph is, wow, well, just amazing. I think I am going to frame it.'

He looked at the paper a few more times before planting a tender and appreciative kiss on my lips.

The sound of revving engines drew gasps from the crowd. The voice over the PA system announced the first race was going to take place in a few minutes, and the noisy cars made their way onto the track. People shouted and cheered as the cars sped onto the racetrack spinning their wheels, causing huge clouds of smoke to drift into the crowd. More cheers and shouts erupted. It did not make sense to me as there was just no possible way for the drivers to hear the noise from the crowd above their car engines. However, I don't think this even crossed the fans' minds at all as they expelled one outburst of exuberance after another until all the cars eventually came to a halt at the start line. Silence fell like a shadow as red lights came on and one by one went off. When the last one went off, the crowds erupted again, everyone jumping from their seats, the cars making a wild getaway to the first corner at speeds I had not ever realised a car could get to over such a short distance. And that was just the first of several races.

Josie and I sat together while the crazed petrol-heads involved themselves with every heartbeat of each race. With every crash or near-crash or even one car's tyres touching another's, the spectators, Egan at the forefront, would go berserk and I had never seen this fanatical frenzied side of Marco or Patty either – it was most amusing.

At midday, while everyone was finishing off their lunch, the voice over the PA system announced that they would be calling out the winning raffle number, and everyone automatically scrambled for their entry ticket.

The number was called out, the crowd hushed, and Josie gave a hesitant grunt, 'Oh dear, that's my number.'

Marco jumped up and screamed with joy while Josie went as pale as the white paint on the track.

'You go,' she said to Marco and handed him the ticket.

Marco made a very feeble attempt to change her mind before disappearing, ticket in hand, to the track where we watched as Jason Mitchell met him. Marco showed him the signed piece of paper and showed him where we were sitting. He waved to us and immediately Egan, Liam and Patty stood up and shouted and waved back while Josie and I sat composedly still.

Marco was kitted out in all the leathers, gloves and a helmet and came back onto the track amid cheers from the crowd as he got into the passenger side of Jason Mitchell's car. Jason's car took off, wheels spinning and Marco's smile beneath his helmet was so broad I was pretty sure we could all see it from where we sat.

The car flew past us going into the corner sideways and then straightening as it came out of the corner. I saw small flames expel from what I presumed was the exhaust pipe. The engine grew louder and louder as the car went faster at every lap.

After the five laps had finished, Jason Mitchell spun the car right in front of us in 360-degree turns, round and round and round until the car became completely engulfed in smoke from the spinning tyres. Egan, Liam and Patty could easily have burst out of their skins from utter elation.

Marco proudly posed for photos with and without Jason and his car before he returned to his seat, embracing Josie not withholding any reservations over what she had given him with a simple ticket. Marco was floating; he was on a cloud of his own still going a couple of hundred miles an hour holding onto every second so as not to forget the exhilarating experience he had just had. He shook hands with all the people around him and gave an in-depth account of his five laps of glory and Egan, Liam and Patty hung onto his every word. Their attention was drawn back to the racetrack at the sound of highly-tuned engines of the even bigger cars making their way around the track. The main race was about to take place, and Jason Mitchell was everyone's favourite for the win.

The race got all the enthusiasts to their feet in the hope of seeing their favourite car and driver and perhaps share in their victory. After just a few laps, all we could see from where we were sitting was a car flying up in the air, at least, eight meters high, flinging bits of car parts in all directions. We watched with our hearts in our throats as the car flung itself into a 360-degree vertical spin before it landed on its roof, missing the passing cars by millimetres. The car rested on the track while officials ran to the wreck. Understandably the officials suspended the race, and everyone stood up again, waiting to see or hear of the driver's safety and to speculated as to which car it was.

After several minutes, there was still no sign of the driver, and soon the ambulance and several other safety vehicles had reached the scene of the accident. Spectators became withdrawn, and there was a grim silence as we all waited for news. Eventually, after at least thirty minutes, the news came over the PA system that the driver of Car Number 31 was safely airlifted to the nearest hospital. His condition was not mentioned but just that the race would continue once the wreck and track had been thoroughly cleared away by the track staff.

Somehow we felt the race would not be the same. Liam and Egan immediately bent their heads and said a prayer and I held Egan's hand and bent my head too, as did Patty, Marco and Josie.

After nearly an hour the race was underway again. The spectators' enthusiasm slowly returned after a few laps, but not to that fever pitch, even when the favourite, Jason Mitchell, won the race. The podium celebrations were cut short, and no champagne was sprayed all over the drivers and their crews. The trophies were handed over, photos taken, and that was that. We left the racetrack feeling very sombre, the air thick and heavy while everyone considered the anti-climax and state of the injured driver. There was no news forthcoming via the PA system since the restart of the race. There was not one driver, car or crew member to be seen on our way out, which only added to the ominous feeling.

While driving home, we heard the news over the car radio – Waylon Stennet, the driver of Car Number 31, had succumbed to the injuries he had sustained from his accident. We listened in horrible silence, saddened to the core and horrified that we had witnessed the last breath of life this man had taken on this earth.

Chapter Eleven

I could not sleep that night. The accident that had claimed the life of the racing driver plagued me. How, after a split-second, we had no more second chances. Where was he now? Was he going to burn in the fires of Hell or would he have eternal life? My mind was in constant turmoil. If I died today, what would become of me? Did I want to be on fire and suffer the pain as described in Hell? What would I do about it?

I decided that before leaving for Patty's on my way to church, I would speak to Dena. Once again I was bitterly disappointed when I walked into Dena's house to find another strange man in her kitchen. At least, this time, he was older than she was, or so I thought. I couldn't help but wonder where she found them.

Dena came waltzing into the kitchen when I was almost out the door. She called me back to introduce me to the gentleman. I told her about the accident and how it was making me reconsider my life. Her reply was, 'You have been hanging around those churchy guys for far too long.'

I stared at her in disbelief, could she be that callous? Even her date just stared at her as I left without uttering another word.

Marco, Josie and Patty were in the same sombre mood as we sat at the kitchen table having coffee and cereal before leaving for church.

'It doesn't help to sit and think about it and think where we would want to end up; we need to act on it. So I don't know what you girls want to do, but Marco and I spoke about it last night, and we are going to speak to Minister Wade after church about getting baptised.'

Josie ended her speech and stared at Patty and me, opening her arms towards us, welcoming us to embrace her. We both did. Patty and I looked at each other and with unspoken words agreed it was what we too had decided on but just needed to have affirmed. Before leaving the house, both Patty and I phoned Liam and Egan respectively, and both got their voicemails and left the same message for each of them – that we had something to tell them before church.

Their curious and confused expressions provided the much-needed humour to make light of what had begun as a disturbing day.

Patty and I said out loud together while Marco and Josie stood by smiling, 'We all want to get baptised today.'

Egan and Liam exclaimed with joy, giving high fives and hugs to us all and rushing us off to speak to Minister Wade before service began.

Not wanting to make a big occasion of it, we decided that the baptism should take place in the sea at Bikini Beach, where Patty and I had spent that wonderful afternoon with Egan and Liam a few months back. The harsh words from Dena when I had told her of my decision still hurt. Was it too much to ask of her to be happy for me? Was it too much to ask her to consider Jesus?

Egan and I floated on lilos in the pool next to each other, my body drenched in sunscreen. He reached over with his hand, smoothing my wet hair from my face.

'Don't worry about your mother; all you have to do is plant the seed – whoa!' Egan's voice bellowed before he could end his sentence as he toppled over and pulled me with him into the water.

It is a foregone conclusion that lilos are untrustworthy, unpredictable and unstable. Make too much movement on them and you are likely to land up underneath them rather than lying on top of them.

We spluttered our way to the surface laughing and wiping the water and hair from our faces. Egan was apologising unconvincingly while pulling me toward him as we kicked our legs in the water to stay afloat and upright. This time, an apology would not cut it. I dug my hands with downward pressure quickly and sharply into his shoulders until he sank below the surface, and then I swam away in haste so as to not be within an arm's reach when he resurfaced. He came up breaking the water surface with a facial expression that had revenge written all over it. It was my turn to shriek as I tried to make my getaway. I felt his fingertips slide across my ankles, his Irish laughter right behind me. I put my feet down and touched the bottom of the pool now able to run the last few paces before reaching the steps. Clambering out of the pool and to the safety of Josie, I hid behind her, laughing as I soaked her with a bear hug.

Men always stick together; that was a lesson I should have learned the first day we met at Bikini Beach. A pair of strong arms lifted me over a shoulder in one swoop, my feet swinging out from under me. At the edge of the pool, Egan took my arms while I still hung over Nathan's shoulders. Then Nathan held onto my ankles, and the two of them swung me sideways over the water and back over the paved edging of the pool and counted to three. At three, I was airborne at least two feet, flying above the water when at last gravity kicked in and I fell towards and through the water spraying a couple of litres out of the pool, my scream dying as the water took its place in my throat.

When I had recovered enough to make all sorts of threats to the perpetrators, I couldn't help but succumb to Egan as he stood on the steps of the pool with a towel and his Irish smile, apologising once more through his thick Irish laugh. Nathan stood not too far behind him, begging forgiveness too, although not as convincingly. Patty was crying she was laughing so much.

Hmmm, so much for an alliance with her.

I looked at the other ladies and found that I was alone in this battle as they were all bent over with laughter.

As the day progressed and we sat under the lapa listening to Egan and Liam playing their guitars, we sang songs and had a jovial afternoon.

Patty wondered out aloud, 'Should we go to the beach? Why don't we just get baptised here, I mean everyone is here already, except Minister Wade?'

There was a hum as everyone discussed what she had just said and no sooner than later we all agreed that it was to be here and not at the beach. Liam phoned Minister Wade, and it was not half an hour later when Minister Wade, his wife Jackie and their daughter Natasha, arrived at the house.

While we mentally prepared for the baptism, Minister Wade confirmed what we were about to do, and we affirmed our understanding and commitment. We all made our way to the edge of the swimming pool and stood in a circle, holding hands. Liam led us in a prayer asking God to accept us into His Kingdom and to guide us as we walked His path in righteousness.

We got into the pool, the water a vast degree colder than it had been at midday. It took my breath away as it reach above my thighs, then up to my waist, forcing me to take short deep breaths to adjust to the cold.

Minister Wade asked us, all the same, questions individually before immersing each of us below the water surface so that our bodies were completely submerged in the water.

Do you understand the plan of salvation?

Do you repent of your sins?

Do you accept Jesus as your Saviour?

We came up renewed; our lives would start new, fresh and with the Holy Spirit guiding us.

Jackie waited with towels as we exited the pool and little Natasha had a gorgeous smile and a plate piled high with cookies. Once more we stood in a circle holding hands and Minister Wade prayed, welcoming our souls to God's family.

I could only speak for myself as to how I felt at that moment even though the others said they felt the same way when they were baptised. I felt a sense of relief, a feeling of being. That I finally belonged to a family in this universe that would always stand by me. I had an overwhelming feeling of completeness and an enormous song of gladness in my heart.

All I wanted to do was scream from the rooftops for everyone to hear that I was saved and that God was my Saviour. If it were possible for anyone to have a smile and a heart happier than mine at that moment, it was Egan. He had been instrumental in my salvation, and it meant that now we would never be unevenly yoked.

Chapter Twelve

On my way to work the next day, everything seemed so much brighter and clearer. Even Dena's verbal abuse of the previous night, on hearing of my baptism, could not dampen my renewed spirit.

'All you can do is pray for her and show her the way by being an example of God's glory,' Egan had said, after witnessing her yelling.

I took courage from him as he had smiled at her and said a polite goodnight to her. It had infuriated her even more.

While my mundane workday pressed on, I couldn't help but examine the faces of my fellow colleagues. They looked lost and worried. I knew that I was still a baby and needed more spiritual food to mature as a Christian and that I was not to judge anyone, but I saw the world and all its inhabitants in a completely different light now.

I wanted to tell everyone I passed, 'Do not worry, God has a plan for you.'

Finally, Alice popped into my office, and I could tell someone my most excellent news. I told her all about my weekend, the unfortunate accident at the racetrack, my decision to be baptised, Sunday afternoon and the moment that had changed my life. She listened curiously, not once being condescending as Dena had been, and I felt confidence grow in me.

Not everyone is Dena; I thought to myself.

Trey walked past my office, noticed Alice and me talking, then immediately back-pedalled to stand squarely in the doorway.

'What's going on? Aren't you supposed to be working?'

'It's our lunch hour,' Alice answered quickly and in a manner that required no reply from Trey or me.

He raised his eyebrows and left. Alice and I just laughed as we went on with our conversation. She was mostly interested in my decision and asked me what had finally made me decide, where I had studied and with whom I had done the studying. And of course, she could not resist finding out more about Egan. I glowed as I eagerly satisfied her curiosity. We sat in my small office which consisted of a desk and a shelf that stood from the ceiling to the floor and which could not breathe for the sake of the files packed into it. The wall not occupied was bare. Not even a single photo or office memo graced it. Planting herself with her back against the wall, Alice's short, extremely slender shape with her dark complexion hung on the wall like a shadow. Her jet black hair made the shadow look even more like an illusion.

'I used to go to church, but since I started going out with my boyfriend Fred, I don't go anymore because he doesn't like it.'

I felt sorry for her as I could relate to her with regards to Dena.

'If there is one thing I learnt in the studies and after that accident at the track, we never know when our last day will be, and the question is, will we be ready?'

Before our lunch hour was up, I told Alice about my relationship with Dena and her reaction to my baptism.

'She, fortunately, is not the one that has to answer for me one day. I will stand alone before God on the Day of Judgment. Liam emphasised this so many times during our studies.'

I hoped I did not sound as if I was judging Alice in any way, and she left to go back to the sales department with the indication that we would continue our discussion soon.

It was wonderfully exciting to talk to Alice, whom before today had not really befriended me. I texted Egan to tell him what had transpired.

His reply was simply: *'God works in amazing and strange ways, perhaps you are the instrument God will use to rescue her soul.'*

My heart fluttered, Egan being so close to me even if it was through cyberspace sent my heart racing with happiness.

I noticed Trey walking towards my office and quickly grabbed my pen, stared at the papers in front of me and with great speed, tucked my cell phone under my legs. He stood in the doorway again, his arms full of papers. His thinning blonde hair exposed the stress lines around his almost black eyes. He had a sharp nose, which although unusually big, suited him. He was taller than me by a few inches but kept a hunched posture that made his nasty character all the more nasty-looking. He always looked as though he was about to pounce on anyone who walked by him. He wore braces instead of a belt, and his shirt was always sloppily half-tucked into his pants in a very annoying fashion. Whenever I was walking behind him, I always had the urge to tuck it in for him.

'Don't take your lunch in the office Vanda, it gives the impression that you are chatting instead of working,' and with that he simply walked away.

My good mood diminished for a few seconds until I heard him curse so loudly that the entire building heard him as he dropped all the papers he'd been carrying.

I giggled to myself, said a quiet, 'Good karma,' and carried on with my work.

As I left the office to make my way home, the sun still shone warmly, even though autumn was starting to arrive.

I texted Egan: *'Meet me @ the tower clock on the beach after work stunning sunset,'* then started my car, put the hood down and embraced the drive.

At the first traffic lights I checked my phone for Egan's reply, it read: *'The group all coming for sunset that okay?'*

As I was already wearing a pair of summery three-quarter pants and a light shirt with flat sandals, going home to change was not necessary, and I was at the beach within fifteen minutes.

Parking at a spot closest to the huge tower clock that stood tall and had obediently kept the correct time for centuries, I sat on the little wall that separated the sand and the paved walkway. I'd left my shoes in the car, and wiggled my toes into the sand that still felt warm under my feet. I could already feel my skin tingling at the touch of the sun on it. I did not have any sunscreen on me or in the car, and just hoped that the setting sun would not be hot enough to burn my sensitive skin. Mr Drake, for one, would not appreciate another meeting interrupted by my continuous scratching, the last episode of that had been bad enough with him threatening to scrape my skin off with a chisel should I not cease the scratching. Just another ordinary day in the Drake line of insults.

My thoughts were gladly interrupted by a kiss on my cheek, arms being wrapped around my shoulders, sparkling grey eyes and an Irish smile.

'Hello, you've been waiting long?'

Not that he wanted a reply as he planted the next kiss firmly on my lips, lingering, welcoming and desiring before slowly releasing my lips from his. If I didn't go completely squint from sheer delight, it would be quite an achievement. The others joined us and, as expected, it was not long before the lads were playing touch rugby while we ladies sat on the little wall chatting about our day, our lads and our lives.

I mentioned my lunch with Alice and asked the others for advice on how to broach the subject again. Katrin mentioned a ladies' breakfast that the young adults' group would be having soon and that I should perhaps invite her. As we discussed the matter further, the sun began to go down, and our lads re-joined us. The conversation about Alice was immediately reverted to cars when a very sporty red car drove past, sending all the petrol-heads into a frenzy.

We cherished one another as we watched the flaming orange ball sink into the ocean through a bright red sky. It was a spectacular sunset.

Chapter Thirteen

All the staff members of Luxous waited anxiously in the main conference room stuck way back on the first floor. The building consisted of two floors, the ground floor the factory and the first floor the offices. Some days the floors and walls would vibrate from all the heavy machinery all working at the same time. The conference room adjourned the kitchen and our staff relaxation room although it remained a mystery as to why it got called that, as relaxation was not an option in this environment. The first floor was divided up into offices for the different administration sections by badly painted and grubby dry walling. Therefore, the office was not very soundproof, which enabled everyone to hear the rantings and ravings of Mr Drake and Trey in their offices on a daily basis.

Like me, no one kept personal mementos on their desks or walls for fear of them being rudely discarded by the monster bosses. I contemplated the idea of putting a photo on the bare wall in my office and decided that I would take the risk. The idea of making a collage of our baptism photos came to mind, and I thought it might also encourage Alice.

The monster bosses walked into the dull and unwelcoming conference room in unsurprisingly bad moods. They had already been at each other's throats for whatever reason, and so there we sat, easy targets for them to vent their frustrations.

My skin began to itch.

Trey sat down in his usual chair, Mr Drake threw his files on the table and remained standing, taking deep breaths.

My skin continued to itch.

He was a greasy-haired overweight old man who reeked of cheap cologne. His most prominent feature was his whiskey nose. It was commonly known as that by all the staff members because of its redness. Whether he did partake in an abundance of whiskey no one knew, but the name stuck.

The production line manager, Jim, was first in the firing line. He got a blasting that shook the walls for an order that had not made the deadline. He sat calmly and quietly while Mr Drake yelled with pointed fingers and when he had the chance to speak, he stood up and calmly said, 'I quit.'

He threw his letter of resignation at Mr Drake, which he had written that morning in anticipation and walked out.

I wanted to scratch my shoulder so badly.

There was a deathly silence in the room; no one dared to utter a breath never mind an actual word. We sat glued to our chairs begging them not to squeak. Mr Drake opened his mouth, and we all cringed. Who was going to be next?

'Just get out of here, all of you. Get out of my sight you useless bunch of so-called employees. You make me sick, the lot of you.'

He picked up his files and left. We all waited until he was gone before we got up and gingerly left the room.

Just a few more months, just a few more months, I told myself all the way back to my desk.

But could I last a few more months? I looked around at the contents of my office, which, if the truth be told, was so very unwelcoming and so incredibly depressing. This job was not helping my career at all and, would this environment be conducive to my Christian life? I pondered along this line of thought for most the day yet drew no conclusions.

While waiting for the highlight of my every day when Egan arrived to spend a few hours with me, I searched some internet sites that offered employment in the events management field. Surprised by the many positions available within my area or at least within a decent travelling distance, I decided to email my CV to a few of them.

'I definitely won't be losing anything by finding better employment elsewhere,' I said aloud to myself as I clicked the submit button for the last time.

Egan listened keenly to my retelling of our miserable meeting and of my decision to seek other employment, during our dinner of mushroom pasta.

'I reckon you're making the right decision. You need to work for a company in your field, and one that appreciates you. In your prayers, ask God to show you the right way, don't do it on your own.'

I wanted to reply immediately but had a mouthful of food and chewed quickly, almost spilling the food out of my mouth. I laughed at myself until eventually I could speak.

'Thank you, but please don't say anything to Dena. If she finds out, she will make sure she's the one who gets me a job so she can constantly remind me that she did.'

'I love you, Vanda.'

What did he just say? My eyes grew large, my smile dazzled and stars flew from my eyes, while I wobbled dizzily on my chair. I was so ecstatic at his words.

'I am so in love with you,' I replied, leaning forward over the kitchen nook to kiss him gently.

'That came out rather suddenly, sorry; it should've been much more romantic than that.'

He blushed sending his grey eyes into a bright sparkle.

'Romantic by whose terms, this is our romantic moment, and it's perfect.'

He picked up my free hand and lifted it to his lips, kissing my fingers softly and tenderly as a gentleman would do most gallantly.

After dinner, we sat on the couch in front of the TV. The nice thing about the couch was that it was not a very big two-seater which meant we had to sit very closely together.

'I'm hoping to extend my working visa here next year so that I don't have to go back to Ireland. It depends, of course, on the big-shots in Ireland. They don't normally allow it, but I'm going to take the chance. We're going to be together forever; you do know that don't you?'

What was the point of speaking? I simply replied with a lingering kiss. As he kissed me back, my heart, my brain, my toes curled with delicious delight, knowing this would last forever. Nestling in each other's arms, we spoke about this and that and nothing in particular until we both fell asleep. A loud bang woke us with a startle – Dena's car door slamming shut. It was two in the morning.

'Guess her date didn't want her to sleep over,' I laughed sarcastically as I put my head on Egan's chest and closed my eyes again.

Chapter Fourteen

The church building was getting chilly as autumn began to make its presence known. Minister Wade's sermon was warm and uplifting and, as always, it lifted our minds and souls in better service to our King.

There was a buzz around the young adults and the junior youth groups as we all met in the activity hall after service. Patty and I amused at the way everyone got so enthusiastic about the annual camp; which was to take place somewhere in the bush at the end of the following month.

'For most, it's the highlight of the year,' Liam said, 'stuck in the bush, studying God's word, camp fires, games, hiking, and just having fun; it's brilliant.'

'As long as you count me out of the games I will have fun.'

Egan laughed, 'Not happening, sorry!'

While Garth went over details of the camp, my mind wandered, and I thought about what sort of games they might play and how much of a fool I would land up making of myself. I wondered if I had just heard right.

Did Garth mention river-rafting?

My ears pricked and I looked at Egan and Liam, who were looking animatedly at each other, their facial expressions clear evidence that I had indeed heard correctly. Apparently the horrified look that spread across my face was highly entertaining; even Patty found it amusing.

'Aw come now, it'll be so much fun, and none of us have done it before either, you'll see, it'll be great!'

I failed to find any comfort in Egan's words, and the dismayed look remained on my face for the rest of the day. Games and river-rafting aside, I was looking forward to this camp, as Patty and I had never done anything remotely like it before. It would be an adventure, of that I was sure.

After the meeting, I went home alone as I had an assignment that had to be handed in by the following Tuesday. If Egan came home with me, I would be too distracted and knew I would never get it done. However, even without Egan there, the prospect of games at the camp was enough of a distraction, so much so that I could not finish the assignment.

Egan might as well have come over.

Dena was watching TV; for once alone at home on a Sunday afternoon although she did have a lot of paperwork in front of her. She looked up at me over the top of her reading glasses; they made her look very intelligent, and she smiled warmly. I felt relief at not having entered a war zone.

'What are you watching?' I asked while plopping myself down on the couch next to her.

'I'm not watching anything; I'm working, what does it look like?'

Her reply was sharp and authoritative as usual, and before another argument could ensue, I pushed myself up off the couch to leave.

'Don't go, stay, have some coffee, the water has just boiled,' she said, her voice softening, almost pleading.

While I made myself a coffee, she closed her files and turned down the TV, a clear indication that she wanted to spend some time with me; a rare occasion and one that I knew I should accept.

'So, what's happening in your life?'

I knew she was being sarcastic and trying to mock me, but I did not allow it to get the better of me. I was determined to have a good visit with her for a change. I told her about the annual camp and all that they had planned for us.

'I would love to be a fly on the wall watching you in all those games and the river-rafting,' she laughed a little, emitting a slight chuckle, actually sounding interested in what I was saying.

'I can't even begin to think of the total mess I'll make in my attempts to keep up with the others. I'm probably going to make such an idiot of myself, so much so that hopefully after the first game they'll ask me to sit out.'

Again she laughed, 'Yes, you've never really been the sporty type. But if you don't want to do it will they force you to?'

'No they won't, but I do at least have to try. The theme of the camp is "Going Together" so I have to be at least an example to the younger kids even though most of them have been a Christian longer than I have.'

I took the chance to invite her while the mood was good.

'On the weekend, a lot of the parents and other people come through to watch the games and for the service on Sunday. Maybe you can come through with Marco and Josie?'

'I'll see, but I doubt it, though.'

I could not expect more than that, but I was extremely happy she did not insult me or turn me down flat out.

'So you do like this Egan lad and his churchy friends?'

'I do love this Egan lad, and I like his friends, yes.'

Mentioning his name I blushed and the butterflies fluttered and scattered all over my body.

'Well, I really must get my assignment finished. Thanks for the chat and the coffee Mom, it was good.'

'If you want me to go over your assignment before you send it off, I'll be finished with this in about an hour then I can do it for you. I'd be happy to.'

'Really? Thanks, Mom. I'll bring it over when I finish it.'

Games and Dena being so motherly, it only confused my head that I could not get around the final touches of my assignment; it only sang a confused melody.

I had a shower, spoke to Egan for a lengthy amount of time and even he admitted Dena surprised him by her actions. Played my guitar for a while and after an hour and a half of working on my assignment, I was still not completely happy with what I'd done nor was I ready for Dena.

She waltzed into my cottage and my study. I had only just finished printing the volumes of paper when she lifted them out of the printer and sat in the armchair in the lounge and began reading, in my opinion, a load of rubbish. I still felt an air of unease about me.

Did Dena want something from me?

She never bothered with theatrics. When she wanted something, she just asked. Did she have something shocking to tell me and was she being nice to try and soften the blow? No, that would not be like Dena either, she never beat about the bush, if she wanted something she got it, no mess, no fuss. I perched myself nervously on the couch waiting in anticipation for her first ever comments on my work, and that included school work.

Page after page after page was scribbled on then tossed to the floor. She gave no hint of being impressed or not impressed or even an inkling of liking or disliking it. I just sat, sipped at my coffee and watched the documentary on Alaska that was on TV. Every few seconds I would glance over to Dena for an indication of her thoughts. She finally moved, cleared her throat and looked up.

'I've made some notes I think might make an improvement, but you don't have to change them if you don't want to. Well done dear, I am impressed.'

Did she say dear? Be still my heart!

Without giving away the complete and utter surprise I felt at her affection, and without falling off my chair from shock I managed to say, 'Thanks, Mom, I appreciate this.'

She even helped to pick up the papers from the floor and to put them back in numerical order.

'What shampoo are you using now?' Dena asked, standing next to me at the kitchen counter as I was putting down the pile of papers.

Shampoo? She wants to know about my shampoo? What have they done with Dena?

'It's organic shampoo and conditioner that I get at the All Natural shop in the mall.'

My reply did not hide my surprised and curious tone as much as the look on my face failed to do.

'It does smell very refreshing, and your hair looks so silky, I don't think I've ever smelled hair that good. Show me what it is please; I'd like to try it out.'

I floated to fetch the bottles of shampoo and conditioner from my bathroom.

Am I in a twilight zone and is this my obnoxious mother?

Giving her the bottles and thinking she would leave immediately I was surprised again because she didn't. She sat in the armchair and read the contents of the bottles, wrote down the names on a blank piece of paper mentioning that she would be purchasing a bottle of each for herself.

'Well, you must finish your assignment, and I must get to sleep. It was nice spending time with you. Sleep tight.'

She gave me a smile and closed the door gently. Fainting would have sufficed at this immediate moment.

Did all this just happen?

I even pinched myself. They say that it is supposed to help you realise that you are firmly in reality. It just hurt.

Patty was silent as she listened to my report on Dena and when it was her turn to comment she had no words. Instead, she questioned my sanity. I can't say I blamed her; it was too good to be true.

I told Egan who said, 'Perhaps the change in your life has made her think about her life. Perhaps she realises that she is going to be a very lonely old woman if she is not a part of your life. Maybe she is threatened by me taking you away from her,' and then he burst out laughing at his philosophy.

He could not believe it either.

Her comments and suggestions were, in all honesty, fantastic, and I amended my assignment accordingly.

Chapter Fifteen

Marco and Josie drove through the enormously large entrance gates of Rio Adventures, the company hosting our camp. The big Overlander trucks stood at a very intimidating attention as they loaded them with our luggage and other necessities. Marco's van had barely come to a standstill when Egan and Liam were out of the car and whizzed off to join those that had already arrived. Patty, Marco, Josie and I got out of the van slowly, walking hesitantly towards the others standing around, not exactly sure of what was going on or where we were supposed to be. Katrin and Tania rescued us from being total outcasts and with them we joined the ever-increasing crowd of highly enthusiastic young adults and teenagers.

While Egan and Liam were loading our luggage, Patty, Josie and I took the chance to use the bathroom – a natural reaction to a nervous state. An elderly gentleman with the kindest and warmest smile introduced himself at the entrance to the building, as Booker, and showed us ladies the way to the bathroom. On the way back from the bathrooms, I recognised a woman from church who was exiting the lift and who greeted us in a friendly voice.

'Hello ladies, hope you're all very excited for your trip.'

My mind was scrambling to remember her name but with no success.

'We are thanks. We've never been to anything like this before. Are you joining us on the trip?'

Before she could reply my curiosity got the better of me.

'I've seen you at church, but I can't remember your name, I'm very sorry. I'm Vanda, and this is Josie, and that's Patty.'

Josie and Patty smiled and said 'Hi,' as I introduced them.

'Yep, I'm Tali and no, I won't be joining you but will be visiting on the weekend. It's so beautiful where you're going, and you're going to have so much fun, especially the river-rafting, it's exhilarating!'

'Hmm, well, I'll probably agree with you on the venue and its beauty but as far as the adrenalin stuff goes I'd prefer to sit it all out, and I think they'll back me up on that too.'

Tali walked with us to the Overlander trucks. The courtyard area overcrowded with people and finding Egan, Liam and Marco proved a bit difficult. A gentleman I recognised as Tali's husband Josh, encouraged everyone via a megaphone to pay attention to the announcement and instructions. Garth took over and explained who would be going on which truck, that it would be a two-hour trip to the Breede River in Worcester and that we would be stopping only once for a bathroom break.

Before we got onto the trucks we held hands in a very squiggly circle and Josh led us in a prayer requesting God for a safe trip and an uplifting camp giving all glory to God. We also prayed for our loved ones at home to be safe until we were all reunited again.

Marco and Josie said goodbye, promising to see us on the weekend. We gathered our hand luggage and clambered up into the trucks and not very graciously either – being a lady had no place in these trucks. Egan had to help me up to the first step; much, very much, to his Irish amusement.

The huge trucks, even though they were in excellent condition, smelled of bush fires, tents and all things camping. The seats reminded me of very old school buses – green with the leather cracked from age – and, sitting down, I wondered how sore and numb my bum was going to be by the time we reached our destination. The truck was not luxurious by any means; its sole purpose was to transport guests to and from a destination on terrible terrains. It was a shell with seats bolted to the floor and with large windows along the sides. The driver and tour guide climbed in with ease, greeting everyone and, of course, asked if we were ready.

No! I offered to myself.

The truck started with a vibrating roar that ran through the floorboards and sides so much so that the bones in our bodies rattled together. Along with the overly hyperactive teenagers, we all clapped and excitedly exclaimed that we were on our way. Egan's enthusiasm was about to burst through his skin; he wriggled in his seat smiling, laughing and rubbing his hands together like a little boy waiting for his pocket money. I could not help but adore this overgrown Irish lad. His enthusiasm and excitement and his love for God were the only medicine I needed.

The big Overlander truck trudged along at a good pace with no respect or concern for our livers, kidneys and other vital organs getting bashed around. It was not long before the guitars were tuned and we sang to the strumming, lifting our already elated spirits. After nearly two hours of driving on a tar-surfaced road, we arrived at the dirt road that would take us to our campsite. The tour guide, Clyde, wisely suggested we pack the guitars away to avoid possibly damaging them on the rough and uneven roads we were about to encounter. He was not far from wrong as the truck dipped and raised and leaned to the left and right and I worried we might not centre again. Our bodies bopped and bumped along in unison with the truck, and I was sure my bum would be solidly bruised by the time we finally came to a stop. All that prevented us from flying around was holding onto the seat in front for dear life. As the massive trees on either side of the makeshift road cleared, we entered the campsite. The truck slowed through the wrought-iron gates and eased to a halt, letting out a final blast of air. Clyde stood up and gave a few final words of instruction before we forced our stiff bums and legs to stand up and move toward the front of the truck. With a jump from the last step to the ground, we finally arrived.

The first thing we all automatically did was stretch our legs, backs and arms and then we were able to absorb the glorious beauty in which we stood. We looked at the main reception and conference building directly in front of the parking area. There were bungalows on either side as well as ablution blocks to the far side of them. The kitchen was to the back of the conference room with an eating hall to its right. It was a very large camp and very neat and clean. To the left, the trees became dense again as they banked the Breede River. There was a cleared and flattened area that served as a barbeque and picnic area just above the river bank. The barbeque was a huge hole in the ground that served as a massive bonfire in the evenings.

It took a little over an hour to get our luggage from the truck and into our bungalows. The women got assigned to the bungalow furthest from the river, and upon entering them, we were invited into a room with eight beds placed neatly in two rows against the long walls, a window resting above each bed with café-styled yellow floral curtains. Although it felt cold on entering, the temperature did warm up after a short while. We were pleased that each bed had a mat neatly laid at its side, a locker on the left and a small pedestal to the right of the bed with a little bedside lamp on it.

We unpacked our bags slowly, having a laugh over everything we inspected. Everything seemed funny to us in our happy state of mind. Patty, Katrin, Tania and I shared the bungalow with four other ladies from the church but that we did not know very well: Mika, Rinia, Beatrice and Emily.

As soon as we were all done with the unpacking, we made our way to the conference room. Coffee and tea with sandwiches filled the hollow in our stomachs since the truck ride had shaken out anything that had been in there. When Egan saw me enter the room he hurried over to make sure I was happy with the bungalow and to describe their bungalow to me in detail. Theirs looked the same as ours, just with different coloured curtains. The conference room – which would be referred to as Maggie for the duration of the camp – was full of chairs scattered around and people were making small circles as they sat with their groups of friends to enjoy the drinks and sandwiches.

Our days comprised of studies that help me to understand so much more of this new life with Jesus. We had special studies for women, for couples, for new Christians; in fact, every aspect of my new life was covered, and I felt so much more mature and so invigorated.

Our evenings we spent mostly around a mesmerising bonfire. With every flame that jumped high, debates were sparked, and our knowledge grew. We told stories and laughed, but the best was when we sang songs beneath the starlit skies enveloped by the cool night air.

The worst part for me was the games and activities, but I felt more comfortable knowing that I wasn't the only one in the group afraid of not looking like the next sports star.

On one particular day – and it goes without saying, that when a bunch of young lads get together, they must play some game –

cricket was the chosen sport; and it also goes without saying that this bunch of lads always insisted on the women taking part too. I had a cricket bat in my hands, which defined as a weapon in my hands rather than a bat. Sven bowled to me, granted it was an underhand throw, but that tennis ball still came towards me at an alarming speed. I closed my eyes and swung the bat into the air, not at all the way Egan had demonstrated moments ago. I felt a thud as the ball connected with the bat. I cringed, too scared to open my eyes as everyone yelled and then seemed to be holding their breaths for a few seconds – then they all burst out laughing.

I slowly opened my eyes only to see Egan next to me ready to give me a high five. I had hit the ball, and it had gone right through the open window, between the burglar bars and had landed on a couch inside of Maggie. While everyone was laughing at my accidental crack-shot, I shivered at the thought of what might have happened had the ball gone a centimetre to the left. I was happy to entertain everyone but for the safety of all concerned, I chose to sit the rest of the game out.

Friday arrived which meant the river-rafting had arrived. All the ladies in the bungalow dressed in seconds with clear eagerness. It was only Mika and me that were dressing hesitantly. As everyone gathered in Maggie after breakfast, Garth called us to attention to announce the teams and the order in which we would go down the river. I held onto Egan's arm and closed my eyes, listening carefully and hoping that we would be in a boat together. I sighed with relief when I heard I would be with Egan, Liam, Patty, David, Nathan, Katrin and Tania. I would be with people that knew how clumsy I was, and if I made a complete fool of myself, it wouldn't be the first time they would have witnessed it.

The truck took us over the worst terrain yet and how it managed not to crash was, in my opinion, an absolute miracle. We missed trees and rocks by mere millimetres, and I held on for dear life, terrified of getting flung out of the window. I had seen even motorcross bikes and rally cars fail on roads such as these.

When we arrived at the drop-off point, the river looked like a piece of cake in comparison to the drive there. Even the lads wobbled once their feet touched solid ground. We stood in our groups and were fitted with the necessary safety helmets, lifejackets and were all given a briefing on what to expect and what to do. It went in one ear and out the other as I stared at the river. From close-up it did not look as picturesque and calm as it had from the truck. It was flowing much faster than I had originally surmised.

Patty and I, being the weakest, sat in the centre with Egan and Liam in front of us. Our guide, John, sat at the back, expertly capable of steering this death trap I hoped. The rubber duck, I just called it a boat – if it went on water it was a boat to me – was perched up on land with its nose in the water, enabling most of us to get in while the rest pushed us until the boat was completely in the water. They jumped in, and John guided us so that we were facing in the right direction, armed and ready with our oars. John barked out orders, and we all dipped our oars into the water and on his count dragged them through the water.

We moved forward slowly as the boat found the current and followed its path; water lapping at the sides as we dipped our oars in unison, dragging them through and up and out of the water on John's counts. The boat gained speed as the current moved faster, rushing us and forcing us to move our oars more rapidly to keep up the pace.

And that is when things got complicated.

The speed at which we were moving resulted in us dipping our oars into the water at random intervals that caused the boat to swerve left and right as it fought against the different strengths. A rushing noise was becoming increasingly louder as the boat moved through the water faster and faster and it got more and more difficult to steer. The boat started moving in its own direction despite our efforts to control it. The water lapped the sides, splashed over onto us, drenching us.

Faster and faster we crashed through the river that was changing from easy boating to an untamed wilderness. The rushing noise grew louder than our squeals and squeaks. We approached the first set of rapids, and my heart sped to the tempo of the moving vessel, but I barely noticed as I focused so hard on just staying on board. At several intervals, we flew up as we hit small but strong waves and in trying to keep my balance and my bum on the seat, I nearly lost my oar several times. I was all over the place, my oar barely touching the water and John continuously shouted instructions. I adhered to none of them; I just focused on staying in the boat.

We moved wildly to the right of the river where the water hastened down a narrow gateway and, at least, two meters. There were huge boulders on either side; jarring out enough to connect with our heads should they so wish. I was airborne for a second, my bum landed on the edge of the boat and then my feet went skyward.

The freezing cold water tasted dirty, and the depth of the river surprised me, the current even stronger than when we'd been on board. I tried to grab onto a rock, a boulder, a log, anything, to stop myself from flowing forward and away from the others.

Where were the others?

Was I the only one in the water?

I tried to steady myself to look around when I felt a hand slide past mine. I tried to grab hold of it. It was Tania who was floating past me, moving faster than I was.

With a loud crash, I landed head first on a boulder - my helmet thankfully protecting me. I grabbed onto the rock forcing my way to the left side where the water seemed shallower, and I could just touch the ground with my toes. Finally, I could look back, and I saw everyone floating along with the current, fighting the water and struggling to gain control of their bodies. There seemed to be a lot of shouting and calling out to one another, and I could distinctly hear Egan calling my name. I looked around for him and finally spotted him on the other side of the riverbank, sopping wet.

John calmly got the boat to the left bank, and those of us there got back on. Then he manoeuvred it to the other side to collect the rest of the soaking wet passengers.

When we were all back in the boat, with our oars and miraculously with no serious injuries other than a few scratches, we tried to figure out what had happened. No information was forthcoming from me; it was all just a blank until I had tasted the water. Laughter expelled from us as we tried to relate what had happened. The exact thing we had all feared had happened, and I just hoped that it had not been my fault. Luckily, however, that could never be determined.

We managed to get to the end of the rapids and the journey without another episode – fortunately, the rest of the rapids were less intense. Finally on dry land, we exchanged stories with the other groups, and I was happy to learn that everyone had dipped on the first rapid.

Definitely not my fault then!

I had a sudden case of déjà vu as Egan's eyes wanted to explode from the thrill of adrenalin. The rollercoaster ride seemed too vivid, and I could tell he wanted to do the rafting all over again.

For the remainder of the camp, the stories went around and around and around, detailing the river-rafting experience over and over again. Our spirits were high, and we felt a kinship with one another as we worshipped God under the blue sky during the day and that same sky, populated with the brightest stars, at night. I knew God, and God knew me.

Chapter Sixteen

For days and weeks after the camp, we continuously spoke about our adventure and our lives just seemed to get better and better as our spiritual lives grew. The only thing that was always the same was Dena. I had so hoped those few hours we had spent together with my assignment had been a turning point in our relationship and her life. However, on returning from the camp, there was the strangely inevitable car in the driveway, and the old Dena was back.

Josie told me all I could do was pray for her, firstly to accept Jesus and secondly to let Him change her life.

Alice had left her boyfriend and had joined the young adults' group. She had started coming to church regularly and discovered that she had the talent to work with toddlers and she began a course to teach them.

Our workplace remained a miserable grind, and I continued to send my CV out at every opportunity. After numerous rejection emails, I finally received an email requesting an interview.

I sat nervously twitching my leg as I waited for Mrs Ridley to finish with her phone call. She worked from home and had converted her garage into an office and workshop. She put the phone down, and I stood up as she walked toward me introducing herself as Glenna Ridley. We shook hands, and she suggested we go to her office. I walked behind her as we made our way from the lounge, through the kitchen to the back of the house where the office was.

We sat on the armchairs and Glenna said, 'So, when can you start?'

I wanted to jump up and hug her; instead, I swallowed my yelp of excitement and smiled broadly.

'I'll have to give two weeks' notice. You did read in my CV that I am still studying and not yet qualified?'

'I have had too many qualified people that think they're too clever; I want someone I can teach my ways. That's why I want you.'

I was at a loss for words.

Was this true, could prayers be answered so easily?

We discussed the ins and outs and even though I would be taking a pay cut, the idea of working with her, in my field, made my salary irrelevant.

Glenna was of average height with brown eyes, black hair and dressed in a combination of chic and hippie style. On most people it would look horribly wrong but on her, it looked just right - married with two teenage boys who were both avid surfers.

When I resigned, Mr Drake threw my resignation letter at me in his disgusting manner and told me to rethink it. When I calmly handed it back to him, he told me to leave immediately and not to waste his time for two weeks. Even though I knew he would react in this manner, it still hurt. I had never done him any harm nor been on the wrong side of him. But, at least, I was leaving and for that I thanked God.

Glenna and I agreed that I would take the two weeks' leave and start with her at the beginning of the new month as originally planned.

Now what to do with two weeks of nothing?

I woke up late, sat on the beach, walked around shopping malls, visited Josie and went out to coffee shops with her, and filled the two weeks in no time.

My last day of leave and the Sunday before I was to start was a cool autumn day, slightly overcast. We were having a barbeque at Marco and Josie's house after church, with the usual crowd of friends and were all sitting around under the lapa relaxing.

Egan and Nathan were strumming gently on their guitars as we listened, chatted or sat quietly absorbing the good company. Liam stood up and indicated to Egan and Nathan to stop playing. We fell silent wondering what was happening.

'Marco and Josie, please may I have your permission to ask Patty to marry me?'

Well, who would've thought?

We were stunned. Patty's face went white then coloured quickly and then she glowed as we all held our breaths waiting for Marco's reply.

'You don't waste time, do you?' he laughed as Josie gave him a light slap on his arm teasingly.

'Yes, of course, you may.'

We held our breaths a bit longer, sporting huge grins. Patty was bright red again. Liam went down on one knee and pulled a ring from his jeans' pocket and presented it to Patty. Josie was already crying.

'Will you marry me, Patty?'

Through her tears of joy, she managed to blurt out a, 'Yes.'

They stood up, embraced each other, elated, while we all finally let out an array of hoorays and shrieks. I hugged Patty so hard she squealed. I was so happy that my best friend, my sister, had finally found such a wonderful man who loved her so much. Patty held her hand out for us ladies to inspect the beautiful white gold single stone ring, sparkling as it rested on her finger. It fitted perfectly.

'Did you have any idea?' I asked when I got a few minutes alone with her in the bathroom.

'No, I was so confused for a minute; he'd been acting so weird the whole day. Oh, Vanda, I'm so happy!'

Tears rolled down her cheeks of pure happiness.

'So, have you even discussed marriage?'

'We've spoken about being together forever obviously, and about how much we love each other. I never thought he'd propose so soon, though, it's only been a few months, but it just feels so right.'

'It is right; it's perfect, I'm so happy for you.'

We hugged each other, inspected the shiny ring again, and giggled with happiness as I embraced her again.

As we sat under the lapa with the night air getting chilly, wrapped up in blankets, I reflected on how in just a few months Patty and I had made these wonderful new friends, met the lads of our dreams and found God.

Where would the next few months lead us?

Chapter Seventeen

Excited, nervous, anxious, and my stomach full of butterflies, I made my way to my new job in a bright, friendly and welcoming office.

Glenna was as friendly and welcoming when I arrived as she had been on the day of my interview. Not wasting any time, we went through the various projects in progress and ones that still needed quotes. I was pleasantly surprised at how in demand Glenna was. I knew this would be everything I could ever ask for in my career.

We worked together for the day; Glenna was patient with me as I found my way around her programmes and filing systems. To add to the comfortable environment, at lunch we were served sandwiches, and though there was a filter coffee machine in the office, we were served coffee as well. While we were having our lunch, I looked around the office. The converted double garage was very airy because of the skylight installed and the large sliding doors. It was one big open-plan office, my desk in the left corner and Glenna's desk towards the centre. There were large tables to the far right full of swabs, papers and other décor items. Along the back wall, the length of the office, there were shelves and filing cabinets. Just outside the office was a small lawn with a few wrought-iron chairs and a table, and on sunny days like today we would sit there and have our lunch as soft music played from inside the office.

Glenna asked about my life and as I told her about Dena she frowned – I was not sure whether it was from disapproval or pity. When I told her about Josie, Marco, and Patty and gushed about Egan, her frown lifted. She told me a little about her life too. She was divorced, and when she'd met Joe, her current husband, he had helped her start her own business. Although they were both business owners, they had a good family life and always put family first before making any major decisions. Joe had a printing company nearby.

The office was even brighter a few hours later when Glenna's sons arrived home from school and came to introduce themselves. They looked like true surfers with their sun-dyed hair and good tans. Sven and Slade were well-mannered and pleasant, but according to Glenna, that disposition did not last very long on any given day.

The rest of the afternoon we spent driving to all her suppliers and to the people she usually worked with so she could introduce me. After four hours of getting in and out of the car and so many different faces, I was quite giddy. I made a point of diarising everyone I met and the name of the company. It'd take awhile to get to know everyone at the drop of a hat, but I was over the moon.

'And so, you think you'll cope here?' Glenna asked as we were packing up for the day.

'I love it! I can't believe it has taken me so long to get out of my previous job, thanks again for choosing me.'

I went straight to Josie's before going home, to tell her all about my first day.

'This is what I need; I don't mind not owning my company if I can work there. It just seems too good to be true.'

'It's going to be just perfect for you, and you will get exactly the right experience for your studies; your boss might even help you with your final practical exam.'

We discussed the possibilities the job could offer until Marco and Patty came home, and I repeated it all to them before eventually leaving for my cottage.

Egan tapped on the door and walked in stealing his hello with a kiss that I could never stop appreciating.

'Want to go to the beach for a bit?'

'Just let me grab a jacket.'

I chattered about my wonderful first day at work all the way to the beach, until we were sitting on the wall by our usual spot under the tower clock watching the sun set.

'You are going to be fantastic at this job; I just know it. It sounds exciting and adventurous.'

'Uhm, adventurous no, please no. Exciting I don't mind, but not adventurous.'

We laughed as the sun sank behind the earth, which in my world revolved in perfect peace.

Chapter Eighteen

The trees stood bare in preparation for winter's arrival. Then winter turned its savage revenge on all who inhabited earth until spring sauntered out the door, leaving it open for the blazing summer heat. A summer so intense, so swelteringly hot, that it felt as though some days the earth was ready to explode.

I shed many layers of itchy skin thanks to wonderful days spent with wonderful friends outdoors, both on the beach and at the racetrack.

Liam and Patty were married by Minister Wade at a small ceremony under the lapa at Marco and Josie's house in the presence of our usual group of friends, Dena, Liam's parents and his brother. The simplicity of the ceremony enhanced the love and happiness between Liam and Patty – so deeply in love with each other as they stood before God asking His blessings on their union.

Josie cried.

Liam's mother cried.

I cried, and so did poor Marco.

Even Dena was touched.

Patty looked overwhelmingly beautiful in an elegant white satin and lace vintage-styled wedding dress. Her hair was loosely curled and with her makeup applied very naturally she looked like a radiant princess. Liam stood so handsome in dark casual pants, a white shirt and a pale blue tie, a smile on his face that kissed the heavens.

Egan had written an Irish love song for them and sang it to them just before they said their vows; he sat on a stool in black chino pants and a white shirt, strumming his guitar and singing his Irish love song from the heart. The song was so beautiful that we were all pretty sure it was also the reason for all the tears. I listened to every chord, every string that he stroked and every note that he sung as he captured me in his web of notes.

Life was the same, and yet it was different. Liam and Patty still lived nearby, we still enjoyed one another's company on any other day, and Egan and I were more in love if that were even possible.

I had learned so much working with Glenna and every day was what I had wished for in a career. We had many successful events and with each one I grew more and more confidence for my final practical that was looming in a few months. Fear had not reared its ugly head yet.

Each day posed some very manageable problems, none of which caused even so much as a stir. I was gliding through this life on a cloud suspended by my faith, and it was inconceivable that there was any form of calamity looming.

When Egan came walking through my doorway one evening, I knew. I could feel it, and I could see it written all over his face. Something was not right in paradise.

'What's wrong?' I asked him before he could sit down, reaching for his arm as if to steady him.

He sat down slowly on the couch, and I eased my way down next to him holding his hand gently, staring at him, trying to force a response out of him.

'What's wrong?' I repeated urgently.

He let out a huge sigh as he stammered, 'Do you remember a while back I said I had asked for an extension of my work visa?'

'Yes,' I replied slowly, recalling our conversation, and preparing myself for the worst.

'Well, it was rejected. They want me back in Ireland by the end of next month.'

He couldn't look at me and instead kept his eyes focused on the floor in front of him. He swallowed several times trying to hold back the lump that I could see was swelling in his throat. I felt the floor open, and my life melting into it.

How can it be happening, it is not happening? Maybe he's just teasing me?

'Are you serious?'

I knew it was a stupid question, but I hoped he would burst out laughing and confirm that he was, in fact, pulling my leg. He looked at me, no longer able to hold back his tears, and I knew this was no joke.

This can't be happening. How can this be happening?

'No, no, no, this can't be true!'

My tears began to overflow; the one thing on this earth that made me truly happy would soon be taken away from me.

Why?

'Why won't they extend your work permit?'

'I can't remember what the man said, I was so shocked. They said something about needing me in Ireland to train other people. I'm not too sure.'

He stared at the floor again, numb.

'What are we going to do?'

He shrugged his shoulders, held my hands and bent his head. I heard a tiny sob escaped from his throat, and all I could do was hold him as we cried together.

This cannot be true.

We remained joined, holding onto each other not wanting to let go. He eventually pulled himself away.

'I have another meeting tomorrow, and hopefully, I can convince them to change their minds. I can't live in Ireland without you.'

He kissed me gently, his lips salty, and he held me tightly again. We sat stunned for a long time on the couch, not able to make conversation but wrapped up in our panicked thoughts. I had to pee, of all the wrong moments I had to go before I burst.

In the bathroom I stood over the basin washing my hands, splashing water on my face to wipe away the tear stains. I took a few deep breaths to try and compose myself as I held onto the sides of the basin looking down into it as if a solution would pop up through the plughole.

This cannot be true; this cannot be happening.

When I finally returned to the lounge, Egan was in the kitchen making coffee. I went and stood next to him and held him around his waist. His arms around me felt better than home. The kettle clicked informing us that the water had boiled, and our attention was required. Egan finished making the coffee and carried our cups back to the couch where we sat with them in our hands and stared at the floor.

Dena walked in, without knocking or a greeting, as usual.

'What's with the long faces?'

'Egan has to go back to Ireland at the end of next month,' I replied, forcing the lump from my throat.

Egan held my hand, still staring at the floor without a word.

'On my word, that's a classic.'

And that was it, that was her extent of compassion or interest in what was to us an emotional turning point in our lives. She turned around and walked out of the cottage.

I burst into tears, this time, more from anger than anything else. Eventually calming myself, with a lot of encouragement from Egan, we once more sat silently on the couch as we finished our coffee.

We tried talking about other subjects like my work, the young adults' group, our Bible study, but it was no use. We kept coming back to how he was leaving and would no longer be able to be a part of everything and a part of me.

'Let's just wait until after the meeting tomorrow before we make any decisions,' Egan said to me as he left much later than usual.

Sleep avoided me like the plague. My mind kept asking the same questions. *Why can't he stay? Why does he have to go? What am I going to do? Why would God bring us together just to tear us apart?*

But when my mind asked these questions I was, even more, restless and confused. My tears were uncontrollable as I lay in bed holding fast to the pillow and the light linen sheet covering me. The bedroom light was off, but the ceiling fan was going round and round on the slowest speed, murmuring in motion offering no reply to any of my questions.

My phone made a noise to indicate someone wanted to chat with me. I knew it would be Egan, and when I looked at it, the message was just an emoticon crying and a red heart. I replied with several red hearts and cried and cried until I fell asleep just as it was time to wake up.

Glenna was horrified when I told her what was happening. I could not keep it from her as my exhausted face, and puffy red eyes gave away any hope of keeping it a secret.

'Vanda, as much as I want you to work with me forever, follow your heart. If that means following it all the way Ireland then you must. I have only ever seen two couples so genuinely and purely in love. The two of you, and my husband and me. You can't give it up.'

As much as I tried not to make my personal problems Glenna's problems, I couldn't help myself. She so openly wanted to help and be a shoulder to cry on. I appreciated her and my job with her so very much.

Will I have to leave this now that I am finally happy doing what I've always wanted to do? It just isn't fair.

It was so difficult to concentrate for the rest of the day. At least having told Glenna meant that I did not have to try and hide what I was feeling, and, fortunately, we were working in the office all day so I could spare any clients having to look at my mess of a face.

Patty's reaction to my news when I phoned was a replica of Glenna's, and it wasn't an hour later when she arrived at my office with flowers to brighten my day. Glenna arranged for sandwiches and tea, and we sat outside around the wrought-iron table discussing my predicament without coming to any conclusions.

Chapter Nineteen

Impatiently I waited until Egan arrived at my cottage. I had specifically asked him not to send me a message or phone me to tell me the outcome of the meeting. I wanted to hear it in person. However, I was regretting my decision as it did not bode well with my anxiety. The messages from Josie, Marco, Patty and Liam, did not help either. I played out several different scenarios in my head, with several different outcomes. But there was only one scenario I wanted, and that was for Egan to stay here with me forever.

I had a shower, dried my wet hair and changed into a comfortable pair of pants and a T-shirt. We would be going to our regular Bible study after Egan came round, and I took out a light cardigan to take along as the evening air was sometimes a little chilly. But that was only sometimes.

I must've walked the entire cottage about six times before Egan arrived. I was so anxious that just sitting on the couch in front of the TV caused me, even more, stress.

I went to the kitchen, boiled water in the kettle, put out the cups ready with coffee and milk.

I went to the bathroom and cleaned it after my shower.

I cleaned my bedroom.

I watered my plants.

I changed the channels on the TV, at least, a hundred times.

I cleaned the kitchen.

Up and down around the interior of my cottage I roamed, waiting nervously for Egan.

When I heard his car pull up my heart stood still after skipping a beat and sending the butterflies racing through me. It wasn't the exciting flutters like when we'd had our first date, these were nauseating flutters. Not able to wait in the cottage any longer, I ran out to meet him at his little Jeep. His face said it all. I needn't have asked him what had happened; I read it all in that expression once again.

'This isn't fair!' I cried as I held him, tears streaming from both our faces in absolute disappointment.

I wanted so badly for it not to be this scenario. He held me and hugged me closer to him, his one arm around my waist, the other holding the back of my head securing me into his arms.

'I'm so sorry; I'm so sorry. I tried everything, I even begged. I'm so sorry,' he cried.

Once we were in the cottage, I sent Josie, Marco, Patty and Liam the news. Their replies were so sympathetic I felt worse as if my world had savagely ripped my soul.

'Let's go to the beach, it'll be better than sitting here in the cottage,' Egan suggested half-heartedly.

We drove to our spot by the tower clock in silence. Once we were walking barefoot on the edge of the ocean, the seawater rushed over our feet as the flat waves trickled with the ebb and flow, did we dare to speak on the subject of his leaving again. He held my hand.

'Would you be willing to move to Ireland?'

I looked up at the sun, bright orange and still very warm and I remembered what Glenna had said to me.

'I can't live where you are not. I have to finish my course in three months' time, though.'

'I feel so awful to want to take you away from everything here. I still can't believe this has happened.'

He sighed and slowed his pace to almost a standstill, kicking at the water.

'I love you, you know that and you know that will never change?'

I stopped walking and turned to look at him. He could not hide the gloom he was feeling at having to leave me.

'I love you too,' I said as I held his face in the palms of my hands, 'we will be apart for a couple of months, that's all.'

We walked a little further before turning around and heading back to the car. The sun had almost set, and our shadows were long and thin, walking step by step with us.

Our hearts were slightly lifted; we went directly from the beach to Bible study. By now everyone had heard our news, and when we walked into Nathan's house, we were surrounded by our caring friends who offered hugs and sincere affection. Studying God's Word allowed our worried minds to rethink our situation.

Who, after all, was in control of our lives?
We prayed, asking God to guide us in making the right decisions. Not the decisions we wanted to be right, but the decisions God wanted us to take. And in everything, we asked to please God.

As the evening moved along, we spoke more and more about what was about to happen. Listening to our friends' various thoughts and opinions, Egan and I both realised that my moving to Ireland could be an exciting adventure, and if God wanted to use us in His works there, then who were we to argue? I finally managed a smile and slowly my attitude changed. Egan's face went from looking stressed and disappointed to enlightened and excited. The sparkle in his grey eyes returned, and even his few freckles came back to life. We had two months in which time we would have to sell his Jeep and find someone to take over the lease for his furnished flat, and that was really about it. He had no other material possessions. I would wait until he had left to worry about my belongings. Josie was happy and sad at the same time, her mixed emotions written all over her face. As I studied her, I realised that I would be leaving the only mother figure I had ever known, and my heart stirred.

Chapter Twenty

'Well, I am not employing anyone in your place until the very last moment. Things could still change, and you might not have to go,' Glenna said after I told her that I had made up my mind to go with Egan to Ireland.

'I am so sorry to do this to you, I don't want to leave you and my work here, I love it, but I love Egan too much to lose him, and I know you understand how I feel.'

'Like I said before, you must follow your heart. Love like yours is too precious to lose.'

Glenna stood up to go back into the office. We had been sitting outside in the cool autumn air for just over two hours discussing my future. I followed her, returning to my desk and I looked around the office as I sat down on my chair; the sad chords in my heart began to stir once again.

Will I ever find a job I love so much again?

At home, I decided I had better give Dena the news before she heard it from somebody else. When I heard her car pull up in the driveway, I went over to her house immediately, before any male guest arrived.

'Hello Mom, how was your day?'

I thought it best first to get a feel for her mood.

'It was fine, what's up?'

'I must tell you something; you want coffee?'

'Yes please, so what's up?' she repeated.

'Egan has to go back to Ireland at the end of next month, and I am going to Ireland after I've finished my course…to live.'

'You are going to run after a man? If he wanted you so badly, he would find a way to stay here. Why should you run all the way to another country for him?'

'Somehow I knew you wouldn't be happy for me. But, luckily it's my decision, and I'm going. My course finishes in three months, and then I'm leaving.'

'Well, once you're gone, don't think you can just come running back when you realise what a fool you've made of yourself.'

'If I did come back I certainly wouldn't come back to you, don't worry.'

I slammed the door shut when I left the house just as a strange car pulled into the driveway; only it wasn't that strange, it looked very familiar, but I couldn't quite place it. I stood to the side of my cottage in the shadows, unseen, where I could see who was getting out of the car.

No ways! It couldn't be! Could it?

I stared with my bottom lip hanging on the floor. Trey was entering Dena's house.

How on earth did the two of them get together and why, oh why, of all the men in the world did it have to be despicable Trey?

He slammed the door behind him after Dena opened it eagerly.

Back in my cottage, I slumped into my armchair, flabbergasted. I could not in a million years ever have imagined that their paths would cross, and he would land up in her nest of seduction. The thought of him being remotely near my dwelling sickened me so much so that the anger of her reaction to my news disappeared and relief took its place.

When Egan arrived, I told him who Dena's latest visitor was, and he was just as shocked as I was.

'You'll be far away from all this when you're in Ireland. We will be happy; I promise you.'

He kissed me, taking with him all my worry and frustration over Dena.

'I got my flight tickets today and also found someone to take over the lease. It's just my car that's left.'

'I had a long talk with Glenna today, she is so positive for my sake,' and then I chuckled remembering her words about replacing me.

'She says she's not employing anyone to replace me until the very last minute, in case things change.'

'I hope she doesn't think you'll get cold feet. I hope you won't get cold feet.'

He put his arms around me as we walked to his little Jeep, and he pulled me in closer, 'I will find a way to come and fetch you if you do.'

'Don't go putting ideas into my head now, making you run after me is very tempting,' I giggled with him, and he pointed his finger at me as though he was scolding me.

I laughed out loud, for a second forgetting about our uncertain future.

We sat in the movie theatre with our extra large popcorn and an extra large cool drink. The movie was a comedy, and we laughed so much while we ate popcorn that I nearly choked several times. The laughter was just what the doctor had ordered after the last few days of being so down.

We walked out of the theatre still laughing and retelling bits of the movie, laughing all over again. The late night air was chilly and the breeze that came off the sea bit right into our faces as we sat on the wall under the tower clock. Birds sat on the shoreline, just sitting not moving at all, at least, fifty of them. It was a strange and yet comforting sight. We just sat and watched them, not moving either.

'I live close to the sea in Ireland, and we'll go to the beach as often as we can. We must.'

'So here is a clichéd question for you – do you think your parents will like me?' I grimaced, hoping he'd reassure me quickly.

'No, probably not. I'm their darling son; no one will be good enough for me, especially not a foreigner.'

I felt my heart sink. I would fly thousands of miles to be with the person I loved only to have his parents not accept me. Would it be much different from what I had now? I felt extremely sad.

We left the beach and headed back to my cottage. I still felt downhearted at the thought of not being approved of by Egan's parents, but he did not seem overly concerned; this made me, even more, worried. I felt even worse when I saw Trey's car still parked in Dena's driveway. I had to brush that thought from my mind or else spoil the evening for good. We sat on the couch and after a few minutes of silence Egan took my cup of coffee and placed both our mugs on the table. He held my hands and looked deep into my eyes.

'What's the matter?'

'Your parents are not going to like me, I might as well take Dena with me, and it'll be like home.'

Egan burst out laughing while I sat there looking confused.

'You're such a gullible lass,' and he laughed even more.

'Okay, so something is rather funny, and I also wouldn't mind laughing.'

It was hard to say anything above his laughter. A few minutes later, after he had to go to the bathroom from laughing so much, he looked deep into my eyes and said, 'Vanda, I love you. Honestly, I do. I can't believe you took what I said about my parents seriously.'

He had to stifle his laughter again, 'My parents will love you, truly they will.'

He hugged me while he tried very hard to contain the laughter that had not yet subsided. I was not sure if I was annoyed with him or relieved. I decided to be annoyed and wriggled out of his embrace landing a heavy punch on his upper arm.

'That was so cruel, why didn't you say you were joking straight away?'

He started to laugh again, funny little tears rolling down his cheeks.

'I am sorry, I should have done, but I honestly thought you knew I was sarcastic, funny sarcastic.'

'No, I thought you were serious, and the thought of having your parents not approve of me was awful.'

He finally got the hint that I was annoyed and stopped laughing, but a smile remained stuck on his face. Every now and again a giggle would pop out.

'They really will love you,' he said, and when he covered me with kisses, I was finally convinced.

Chapter Twenty-One

Trey's car was parked in Dena's driveway almost every night in the weeks following. I had not yet decided if I was happy that she had one male visitor instead of the constant runway of suitors or if I was angry that it was Trey. So far I had managed to avoid him and wasn't even sure if he knew I was Dena's daughter. It was not like she kept photos of me in her house to give it away.

We were having a farewell dinner for Egan at Marco and Josie's house under the lapa – everyone's favourite social gathering venue. Putting on a pair of jeans, black boots and a black jersey and jacket, I couldn't help but wonder what my life in Ireland would be like in comparison to my life now.

Will I make friends easily? Will we find a group of Christians as dedicated as we have here? What if things go wrong there, and I have to come home?

The lapa had been made up with photos of Egan that we had all collected during the time we had known him. I could sense that this gesture sincerely touched him. People from the young adults' group, as well as other friends and members from the church, were all crammed around the backyard and under the lapa. Liam and the other lads kidnapped Egan from me and dragged him to the fire. I went looking for Josie and found her in the kitchen, where there was a constant hum of people filing in and out, carrying food and crockery on their way to the lapa. She took my hand, and we sneaked away into her bedroom. She closed the door, shutting out the noise the rest of the guests were making.

'What's going on?' I sounded as confused as I felt.

'I want to show you what Marco bought Egan as a going-away present.'

'He did what?'

'I know, I couldn't believe it either.'

Josie opened her cupboard and took out a navy blue rectangular box, the size of a toddler's shoebox. We sat on her bed as she slowly opened the lid, carefully putting it down next to her. She gently lifted out a small replica of a racing car. While Josie understood the value of such a little car, I did not. To me it looked like a dinky toy car, nothing more and nothing less.

'That's it? I thought you were handling a porcelain doll they way you took it out.'

'Read the box.'

I picked up the box and turned it onto its side and read the inscription.

"Limited Edition Replica Race Car Number 31 – In memory of Waylon Stennet."

'Oh! Wow, this is very special. Egan's going to be in his element.'

'There were only ten made in the world. Marco bid for this one.'

'Oh, Josie, please don't tell me he paid a lot of money for it, that wouldn't be right.'

'That's Marco's business. He's so happy he can't wait to give it to Egan; to see his expression!' Josie giggled in delight, clearly as excited as Marco was.

'He should've kept it for himself.'

Josie got up and went to Marco's cupboard, opened the door and took out an identical navy-blue box and held it in front of her face grinning.

'He didn't!' I exclaimed and laughed at the same time.

Josie carefully put the little car back into its box and put both boxes back in their place in the cupboards. Then we returned to the party, trying very hard to conceal our secret.

I found Marco, put my arm around his waist and tugged him into a half-hug and kissed him on the cheek. He looked at me confused and then he figured it out because he smiled at me and gave me a proper hug.

Minister Wade suggested we hold hands as he blessed the food, but before we could start eating Marco asked for everyone's attention. Egan was asked to stand next to him, and he did so sheepishly. Marco spoke about how he had first met this gangly foreigner who hardly spoke English properly, but, how like the rest of us, he had grown to like and even to love him. Josie handed Marco the box Marco handed it to Egan.

'We don't want you to forget us, so this is for you to remember us by...' he trailed off as Egan opened the lid.

Before he had it off properly, he let out a loud Irish, 'WHOAH!'

He gently took the little car out of the box and exclaimed over and over again,

'Oh wow Marco, oh wow, thank you. Wow, I don't know what to say.'

The lads began to cheer, 'Speech, speech, speech!'

Egan stared at the little car, overwhelmed with his gift and with great difficulty managed to say, 'I don't know what to say. This gift is just…wow! Well, um, you all know I don't want to leave, and I'm sorry I'm stealing Vanda away from you all but…wow this is…this is incredible.'

He stared at the car again, and everyone just burst out laughing. And that was Egan's speech. The lads gathered around him all wanting to get a look at the little car, chattering away in their car language.

Patty, Josie, most of the ladies and I sat next to the fire watching the flames bounce up into the air, the lads still inspected the car so we waited for them so that we could eat. We eventually ate, but the lads were still talking cars.

Chapter Twenty-Two

The airport always seemed such a daunting place to me. Some travellers rushed willingly to their destinations; others dragged their feet. Some looked utterly elated and others, like me, wished they did not have to be there.

Egan handed his passport and flight details to the check-in assistant. He loaded his luggage onto the ledge, and it was weighed, approved and nudged onto the conveyer belt to make its way to the waiting plane.

His seat was confirmed and also his meal preference.

The boarding pass was printed and handed to him along with his passport.

And with every step of the process, my heart sank an inch further.

He turned around from the check-in counter, put his boarding pass into his passport and put both in his pocket. He gently put his arm around my shoulders and tugged me close to his side, kissing my cheek softly. I fought to keep the tears from flowing and just smiled back at him.

We went up the stairs to the restaurant area and found the rest of our friends waiting. Patty came to me immediately and said she needed to go to the bathroom. Her eyes pleaded with me to join her. Being the lifetime friend that she was, she could instantly see I was near breaking point.

I stood in front of the basin, turned the water on and splashed my face a little; soon it was not clear what was water and what were tears.

'My biggest fear is that when he gets to Ireland, I'll be forgotten. It can happen so easily!'

'I'm sure it can, but I doubt it will. That man is honest and true and loves you.'

Patty passed me a few sheets of the paper towels, but they were hard and scratchy and made my tear stained face look worse.

'In a few months, you'll be together again, just keep thinking of that and your new life with him.'

She continued to help wipe away my flowing tears.

'Come now, let's get back to them, you don't want to be spending these last two hours in the bathroom and not with him.'

I gathered my thoughts and got my emotions in check as we made our way back to the restaurant. Egan wiggled his way on the seat until he was sitting right next to me and gripped my hand tightly under the table.

Without fail, the men spoke about cars while we ate hamburgers and sipped on our drinks. I was grateful they were there, for they made me laugh, they made the tears move away from their tear ducts and the lump in my throat slither away. Egan spoke eagerly of his country and encouraged everyone to come on holiday to Ireland. When he told stories of Irish car races, and he even suggested the best time of year to visit to watch the best races it was enough to convince them. It was a grateful distraction and for once, listening to them talk about cars was enjoyable.

Throughout the two hours, we spent sitting in the restaurant, Egan sat almost on top of me, and when he wasn't using his hand to talk or to eat, he was holding my hand tightly, planting kisses on it and looking deeply, lovingly, seriously into my eyes. I could see he was trying to assure me that it would all be okay, that everything would work out soon enough.

The voice over the PA system announced far too soon that the passengers of his flight were to board at Gate Six. One by one, Egan was greeted by our friends until it was only me left. Everyone considerately made their way toward the airport exit while I walked with Egan to the boarding gates.

'Just think, next time we see each other you'll be on the other side of the gates, and I'll be on this side waiting for you.'

He put his arms around me, and I knew from the thick words he spoke, he was fighting back the tears as much as I was. I preferred not to say anything to Egan; it was safer so instead I just held him closer, and slowly he released me and kissed me a last goodbye. That went down in history as the longest, saddest and most difficult goodbye kiss - in my book.

He was the last passenger and had to rush his way through the boarding gates to avoid missing his flight. He kept turning around to look at me, smiling, waving and blowing me kisses. I kept looking for my Irish lad dressed in jeans, a grey T-shirt, denim jacket and black sneakers. I kept looking for my heart. Other passengers were watching us; the security officers were watching us, but we did not care as we tried to get that last glimpse of what our hearts longed for most. Then Egan turned, and he was gone, and I was suddenly very afraid.

Is this the last time I'll see him?

I stood alone surrounded by strangers, staring at the boarding gates, wishing he would walk back through them back to me. It felt like I stood there for hours, waiting, but he never did.

I walked back up to the restaurant area holding the warm coat I had taken off when the airport had become hot and stuffy. Finding an open seat by the window facing the runway and near to his plane, I ordered a glass of juice and waited, watching his plane fixedly hoping to get a last glimpse of him. The stairs gradually were drawn away from the plane, and it began to move backwards. I hoped that if I could focus hard enough, I would see him sitting at his window. I hoped in vain. The plane disappeared down the runway. I still stared out the window until it came back into my vision, gaining speed for the take-off. It went by me, and I waved a last goodbye. Then its nose lifted, pulling the rest of its body up with it into the sky. I stood with my head against the window, straining to keep focused on the plane until it was no longer visible.

Will I ever see Egan again?

I picked up my coat and my bag, paid for my juice and left the airport. My feet were heavy with the weight of my heart buried in them.

Glenna was not in the office when I walked in, and I slumped into my desk. There were only two hours left of the day, and Glenna had said I could have the day off, so I left again and drove to the beach by the tower clock. I sat on the wall for a while until the wind picked up and it became unpleasant. Then I drove to Josie's.

Josie was on her way out when I arrived, but rather than leave and go to my empty cottage, I lay down on the couch and waited for her to return. Before long, my eyes closed and I was visualising Egan's face, his sparkling eyes, his Irish smile. I could hear his voice comforting me, telling me that the time would go by so quickly that when I open my eyes again, I would be with him once more and forever this time.

A banging noise woke me up with such a start that I sat up straight like a puppet pulled by a string, and for a few seconds, I was not sure where I was. I saw Josie walking towards me with two cups in her hand. She sat down beside me placing the cups on the table in front of us. I looked at the window with the curtains drawn.

'What time is it?'

'Eight-thirty, you were in such a deep sleep I didn't want to wake you.'

Josie had a soothing voice that could calm the storms.

'Jeepers! How did I sleep so long?'

She never answered me; it wasn't necessary and rather than go home and face Dena, I stayed the night. Marco, in his usual happy mood, helped to get the first night without Egan behind me. It was a strange and uncomfortable feeling knowing he wouldn't be walking through the door at any minute. I missed him. I missed him so much already. Thank goodness for technology.

Chapter Twenty-Three

It was hard to comprehend how I would ever have been able to put together the event for my final practical exam if I had still been working at Luxous. Glenna assisted in every way possible, allowing me to use one of her clients. She made all her resources available to me, as well as allowing me to use my working hours to put it all together. Her kindness and generosity made me feel so guilty about leaving. If only I could take this company and my job with me to Ireland.

On top of the fact that I was extremely busy, I was constantly irritated, and my head was either foggy or nauseous. I hoped a boost of multi-vitamins and anti-allergy pills would help until after the event, and then I would see a doctor and get proper medication.

The event was for a hair stylist competition – a most unusual event and one that I had never heard of or that Glenna had ever done; we were both very excited. It brought its challenges with it, and we were exposed to a whole new industry – from the stylists and the hair itself to the rules, unique procedures and the products. The competition was open to the local hair salons in the Helderberg region, and each salon was permitted one entry. The funds raised would go to the local children's shelter, and the winner, crowned as the Helderberg Hairstylist of the Year would go through to the National competition to be held later in the year.

With one week to go, there were nine entries and I was more than happy as too many would be difficult to control and too few would just simply be boring. There had to be a panel of five judges which, fortunately, with the help of the stylists, was easy to arrange. Each contestant had to create an original hairstyle using whatever products and accessories they wished, and they had one hour in which to complete the styling. Then the model was dressed in a chosen outfit that set off the intended creative theme, and the completed look then modelled for a final judging.

All the sponsors, ranging from shampoo to accessory companies, flooded our office with samples and free gifts for spectators. I got Josie and Patty and even Dena, to help one Saturday to make up gift bags and placed one on every seat. We still had so much left over that I managed to convince the lads to walk around handing freebies out to passers-by on the day.

As the day of the competition drew nearer, the media got more and more involved – interviewing the contestants, the judges and the organisers, including me. It was an absolute first for me, and I was so nervous that I stuttered and fidgeted terribly. The nauseating feeling intensified, and I thought at one stage that I would throw up.

I was living on about three hours of sleep a day, and it suited me not having the time to wallow and be depressed about Egan. I missed him terribly even though we were constantly sending each other messages, all day and all night long. For at least an hour every night, we would speak to each other via a video call, which made the longing so much more.

Everything I did for the competition I recorded and, in some instances, photographed, for my final practical exam submission. I also had to submit a portfolio of all the events I had done previously, as well as a CV and referrals. Since I had to hand it to the assessment critics at the competition, this added an extra load to my already overloaded schedule.

Stepping out of the shower, I felt refreshed but still exhausted and at least, for now, was not sneezing or nauseous. All I wanted to do was collapse on my bed, but Dena walked in and put the kettle on as she yelled at me from the kitchen to let me know she was there. It was late, and I didn't have the energy to fight with her, so I put on my gown and slippers and went to the lounge. I cuddled up on the couch and threw a blanket over my legs. Dena placed our cups on the coffee table and sat in the armchair. I waited for her to speak.

'How are the competition arrangements coming along?'

'Good, I hope. Glenna thinks I have everything covered.'

'It's a fascinating event. Something very unusual, it should create a lot of public interest.'

'It has, it truly has, especially since our little towns have never had anything like this before. The thing that scares me most though is the media. At this level there are no TV cameras, thank goodness, but the press is scary enough on its own.'

'Well done, Vanda this is a great achievement for you and if you don't get 110% let me know who your critics are and I will sort them out.'

She giggled, and I wanted to choke on my coffee. Dena was making a joke and, best of all, she was in complete support of my career choice.

'I will get their names and addresses for you in advance, just in case.'

'Trey, he was your boss at Luxous I believe?'

I couldn't believe she was talking to me about him. I cringed.

'You mean monster boss. Why do you ask?'

'Well, you might have noticed that I haven't been seeing anyone else besides him for a while now. I in fact like him.'

'Really?' That was all I could say; I was too gobsmacked at the thought of anyone liking him.

'I know you think he is nothing short of evil, but he isn't like that with me. He's quite the gentleman.'

'It cannot be the same person then. We're not going to do the whole getting-to-know-each-other thing are we?'

'You know I don't do all that, so just relax.'

We sat in silence for a few moments and then she spoke again, Miss Chatterbox for a change.

'Is there anything I can help with on Saturday?'

Now, why can't she always be like this?

'Thanks, Mom, that would be great there is usually always something that requires additional help.'

'I'm keen to see the outcome, you know, when they're all dressed up, there's quite an art to it.'

I agreed, and, for another hour, in which I could've had some much-needed sleep, we chatted about the competition, hairstyles and themes. The evening, in particular through the last two hours, were probably the best two hours I had ever spent with Dena, and it confused and delighted my already tired mind.

Before falling asleep, I sent Egan my usual goodnight message and also gave him a brief description of Dena's visit. He sent a confused emoticon back and a sweet, good night message.

I wrestled with sleep. My dreams were full of hair – hair catching on fire, hair being dyed the wrong colour, models looking like freaks with nests on their heads, some with no hair at all. I dreamed of a poor turnout and that those who attended found the whole event terribly boring. I dreamed that the judges didn't pitch and then that the contestants didn't pitch. I dreamed there was a power failure. Then I dreamed the electricity came back on, and I tripped over a cable and disabled the power supply. Then I bumped into someone and caused a domino effect that sent contestants and models stumbling and ruining everything in sight. In another dream, the critics were not impressed with my effort and my work, and I failed. In another one, I left all my paperwork for submission somewhere, and I rushed around in vain trying to find it.

There were no positives running through my mind, only every scenario that could go possibly wrong. I tried to sleep. I tried to think of the positives. I tried to think of Egan. I tried to envisage Ireland. I remained restless and woke up more tired than before I'd gone to bed.

Chapter Twenty-Four

Glenna was by my side every step of the way, not interfering but just assisting and advising me. Having been through it all herself she knew the magnitude of the occasion.

I was the first one to arrive at the hall on a chilly winter's morning. The rain had been kind and was not supposed to put in an appearance until the following day. I put my files down on my little desk, which was in the corner of the hall behind a side screen so as not to clash with the décor or the competition itself. With my checklist under my arm, I wandered around the hall inspecting each stand, thoroughly checking the contents against the checklist given to me by the judges. I also made sure that their score sheets were placed neatly on their table.

The entrance to the hall, beautifully adorned with an archway covered in hair accessories, and to the left on the inside of the hall was a table covered with a tablecloth printed with hair combs. On this table, there were programmes and a box for charity donations, a clipboard with raffle sheets and a lockup box for the raffle and charity money. Once guests showed their tickets, their wrists ceremoniously got stamped with the date and the name of the competition.

Patty and Josie had kindly offered to take on this responsibility for the first shift. All the volunteers came from my group of friends and the hair salons' staff and their families, and everyone worked in half-hour shifts so that they could all get a chance to see the competition in full swing.

While I waited for the contestants and volunteers to arrive, I walked around the hall again and made sure every seat had a gift bag on it. I was fussing like a mother hen checking up on her brood, and I grinned to myself at the thought. I stood and looked around at the hall, the décor, and the stands with all the equipment and I had a sudden pang of sadness in my heart as I wished Egan was around to see my handiwork.

He would've looked around, nodded his head and with his huge Irish smile have said something like, 'Ah, fair play love, well done.'

Then a pang of panic hit me and all the horrible thoughts that had kept my sleep from accompanying me last night, came flooding back. With them in mind, I quickly checked on the cables that ran from the stands to the main switchboard to ensure they were in fact firmly stuck on the ground and that no one could trip over them, especially me.

The entrance door opened, and I was so relieved to see that it was Glenna. I greeted her and gave her a rundown of everything I had already done before she even had a chance to open her mouth. She went over everything with me and once she said it was all okay I relaxed a little, just enough for the panicky feeling to subside, and only my nausea lingered.

Soon contestants and volunteers began arriving, and I no longer had time to think of things that could go wrong. The judges arrived, walked around the hall and inspected each and every stand to ensure they conformed to the rules of the competition.

About half an hour before the doors were opened to the public, the two critics who would be judging me arrived. That panicky feeling crept back and nervously I showed them all the paperwork and the portfolio they needed to see, and I gave them a tour of the hall set-up, collaborating everything with my reports and spreadsheets.

I felt sick.

They neither smiled nor frowned.

What were they thinking?

It was time to open the doors and to let in the waiting people. I gasped as I saw the queue of people waiting to get ushered to their seats. Liam, Nathan and David waved at me showing off the products they were handing out to passers-by. I smiled and waved back, blowing them a kiss. They seemed to be having a really good time interacting with the crowds of people.

Spectators seated, contestants positioned at their stands, and the judges hovered among them, armed with their clipboards. The mayor stood on the stage with the microphone and a bell. She gave a brief speech and wished everyone well. Glenna and I held our breaths, and so did every other person, including all the volunteers.

She rang the bell.

It clanged, and the guests cheered while the contestants went to work instantly, their fingers like little machines attacking the models' hair. In one hour they had to create magic. Then the models under supervision would disappear to complete the overall look and come out to model the creations. The smell of hair products soon began to consume the hall, not helping the feeling that was swimming in my stomach.

'Maybe you should get the top windows opened to help release the fumes and smells?'

I looked at Glenna and knew she was right, of course, she was right, and I dashed off to the head security officer. He was a tall man, his black uniform seeming to extend his height by at least a few inches. He had a rough face, his black hair showing signs of greying at the temples and yet he spoke with a gentle voice and his shy eyes lit up.

'Could you open the top windows please, I think the fumes and smells might become too much before long?'

He looked up at the windows and around the room and nodded, 'Will get right on it, Miss Vanda.'

And he disappeared in a flash as I went back to the side screen by my desk and stood once more next to Glenna.

'Thank you, thank you very much.'

Glenna put her arm around my shoulders and rubbed my upper arm smiling. 'You've done very well, now stop stressing.'

'When I finally see a smile on the faces of those two critics then I might finally start to relax.'

'That's the way they are. They always do this, not giving away an inch of what they are thinking. They've done it like this since my days. I think they're a special breed of people, those critics.'

I had to laugh at her.

Music filled the hall and Joe, the Master of Ceremonies, walked in between the contestants asking them questions about what they were doing but getting only very vague answers. However, not deterred he would just turn his attention to the judges or the spectators or even to the owners of the hair salons represented.

It was so fascinating to see what incredible trickery the hairstylists used and what they could do with a simple head of hair. I had no idea or even the slightest inclination that hair could be bent, twisted, stretched and curled into such magnificent angles.

A tap on my shoulder startled me, and I turned to see Dena standing next to me.

She had come! Dena had come to see something that involved my career.

'This is all so fantastic and so interesting.' Dena said, staring in amazement at the contestants spraying and twirling and manoeuvring the models' hair, with fingers like tentacles.

'Thanks so much for coming, Mom, this is Glenna, Glenna this is my mother, Dena.'

They shook hands and exchanged pleasantries.

'I must find my seat dear, so I will probably see you afterwards then.'

Did she call me dear again?

Glenna and I did not discuss Dena once she had left; instead, I took another stroll around the hall spotting Minister Wade and Jackie, Tali and Josh and Garth and Merle all sitting together. They greeted me with bright smiles, and all gave me thumbs up. Then I went on to the contestant area checking once more that every need was taken care of, and then I wandered in between the spectators, ensuring they were comfortable, happy and still interested.

I noticed the critics sitting watching the competition, their clipboards nowhere in sight and I wondered whether that was a good or a bad sign. The contestants seemed to be moving their fingers even faster as the time edged closer to the one hour mark. Hair sprays fumed in plumes, and I was very grateful for Glenna's suggestion earlier as I sneezed several times from the fumes creeping up my nostrils. Even my eyes began to water.

I could see the contestants were beginning to feel the pressure, they constantly glanced at one another, stealing with their eyes, then refocused on their tasks at hand. Hairdryers were singing, and the heat circled the hall as it was a hot summer's day. While sitting in their seats, spectators bobbed their heads from side to side trying to get better views of what the contestants were doing. Now and then an 'ooh' or an 'aah' could be heard as a contestant achieved an impressive look.

The media photographers were endless in their pursuit of the perfect photo, which would capture the perfect moment and expression of contestant and model, or if they were lucky, both. The ten-minute announcement sounded. Fingers flew faster, the audience murmured curiously and shifted in their seats not wanting to miss the final few minutes.

The five-minute announcement echoed over the noise. Fingers flew even faster if that were even possible. Final touches hastily added to what looked like masterpieces, every one of them.

The one minute call came over the speakers.

The five-second countdown was loud and clear and the audience helped count down, 'Five, four, three, two, one!'

'Stop!' yelled Joe the Master of Ceremonies, and the mayor rang the bell once more.

The audience cheered and clapped and the contestants looked exhausted as they put down their equipment and took a full look at what they had created. Contestants scrutinised one another's work, wondering if they got preferred above the rest.

The security officials escorted the models to the dressing rooms where they would change costumes to complete the desired effect. The spectators eagerly chattered among one another, swapping opinions on each entry and trying to decide who they thought would be the winner. There was a loud hum as the audience became more and more excited. Joe could have caused them to riot had he wished to do so, they were that excited.

I went to the changing rooms to make sure all was in order. The judges were standing by making notes, so I left, realising I would probably just get in the way. Returning to the side screen and Glenna, I felt my phone vibrating in my pocket and my heart leapt as I read the message from Egan: *'Liam tells me it's a huge success. Wish beyond wishes I was there. Well done my love and I won't say I told you that you would do great. I miss you like crazy and love you xx.'*

I held the phone to my chest and closed my eyes.

What I wouldn't do to have Egan with me right now.

The judges came back from the change rooms and once again took their seats at the table facing the stage. The MC asked the spectators to calm down as the moment we had all been waiting for had arrived. He thanked the sponsors, the competing hair salons and the judges, as well as the spectators, for what had been a wonderful competition and what was now a first in the Helderberg area and hopefully not the last. He wished all the contestants luck as they showed off their final creations.

The models were brought out onto the stage by their hairstylist. They walked about the stage showing off their outfit and hair to the whistling and cheering crowd and to the judges who were, at last, smiling. The outrageous hairstyles and themes ranged from Egyptian, Martian, Retro, Bridal and Floral to Techno, Vintage, Futuristic and Elizabethan.

Every model looked spectacular.

The crowd cheered and whistled and clapped for each model as she displayed herself like a peacock showing its glorious feathers with pride. Finally, all the models stood together in front of the judges alongside their stylists. The head judge walked up to the stage while Joe introduced her. She thanked the contestants and the spectators and handed an envelope to Joe.

The drum roll reverberated over the speakers and people fidgeted in their seats. The contestants and models looked anywhere except at the judges while trying to control their nerves. Joe slowly opened the envelope, holding the microphone at the same time so that the audience could hear the envelope being torn open. He took out the card that revealed the name of the second runner-up.

'Jordie from Calypso with her model Kate the Egyptian!' he yelled, and the audience yelled back, and wild clapping ensued. Then the drum roll rolled over the speakers again, and Joe hesitated, smiling, feeding the people all the suspense they wanted.

'The first runner-up is,' there was a dramatic pause, 'Bernie from Heads with his model Ann the Techno!' Joe's voice escalated with every word.

The crowd erupted and after several minutes of noise, the moment had arrived. The remaining contestants were possibly more nervous, and all held hands, knowing that it might just be them that could be holding the trophy in the next few seconds.

Joe picked up the trophy.

'Who do you think this belong to?' he called out, and the spectators, officials and volunteers went mad.

They yelled back the names of their favourites so loudly that to me it just sounded like one big clap of thunder.

'And now, for the moment we've all been waiting for!'

Joe hesitated.

'The winner of the Helderberg Hairstylist of the Year is…'

He hesitated again causing a frenzy of response.

'The winner is…Cheynne from Moments with her model Peta, the Vintage!' He held the trophy, the envelope and the microphone high up in the air. Cheynne and Peta screamed and hugged each other while all the contestants crowded around them trying to hug them and congratulate them all at the same time. Joe had to fight his way to the winners as silver strips of paper flooded the stage from above. The crowd of people had by now stood up the shouting, cheering, whistling and clapping getting louder. The winners held up the trophy with their salon owners and representatives who had rushed up onto the stage at the announcement.

It took, at least, two hours for the last person to leave the hall and, during that time, the two critics came up to me and informed me that I would receive my results within forty-eight hours. Still no hint of a smile. It was rather unnerving.

The cleaners arrived, and the tall, head of security man assured me that I could go and leave the rest to them.

'Miss Vanda,' he said with a slanted smile, 'that was the best show I have ever seen here, it was very exciting.'

'Thank you, I truly appreciate it.'

I left the building alone just as I had arrived, how many hours earlier I couldn't remember I was so tired. My eyes were burning from the hairspray fumes and the sick feeling in my stomach had never left.

Trey's car was in the driveway when I got home to my cosy cottage, which didn't help my nausea but I still made a video call to Egan and retold the entire day, even though I was so tired, I would not give up the time with him. Talking and seeing him, even though it was through a laptop screen, made my day and every other day complete.

I so longed that he was with me. I missed him so much.

Chapter Twenty-Five

Glenna and I sat in the office with the rain pouring down in thick heavy drops, making a constant tapping sound against the roof and the big sliding doors. We had no desire to do any work but rather shared what had happened on Saturday and our feelings and thoughts on the event. We were constantly interrupted by the phone, and almost every call was congratulatory. It was already Tuesday, and the calls hadn't stopped. I felt on top of the world but was too afraid to get completely happy until the final results arrived and I saw the word "passed".

If my nerves were not bad enough, almost every hour, I received a message from Egan. He would ask if I had received the results yet or would say that I shouldn't worry as he knew I had passed or he'd simply say, 'I love you'. That was a message I was willing to read over and over again.

The rain was falling even harder, and the skies had become dark and thunderous. Glenna, fearing that the conditions would get even worse and possibly that the electricity would trip, suggested we called it a day.

Snuggled under my warm feather duvet, I was grateful for the terrible weather, as perhaps now I could, at last, get some real rest and get rid of the sick feeling I could not shake. I clutched my phone in my hand waiting for it to vibrate to let me know that I had received an email.

When I woke up four hours later, it was only five o'clock in the afternoon. It was dark as midnight and the rain, joined by thunder and lightning, had not eased up at all. The first thing I automatically did was check for any emails, one in particular. The only emails were from clients and the regular marketing emails that I hardly ever read. Bitterly disappointed, as I so desperately wanted to get my results so that I could finally get to Ireland and be with Egan once again and this time forever, I pulled the duvet over my head and sent Egan a message.

Dena woke me up two hours later, and still the rain belted down, perhaps even harder than before. The electricity had in fact gone out due to the storm, which was the reason Dena had a torch shining into my face causing me to blink and squint from the light.

'Why did you come here in this weather?'

'I tried phoning you, and you never replied, and I wanted to know if you had your results yet.'

'Nope, nothing yet.'

'Oh well, I'm sure you'll get them tomorrow then.'

She left, and I got out of bed and made my way to the bathroom with the dull light from my phone. In the process, I banged one, or maybe several of my toes against the leg of the chair in the room. The pain was riveting, sending a message through my entire body that little toes have feelings too. My foot was too painful to step on, and I was forced to hop to the bathroom in the dark. I found the toilet and sat on it phoning Patty, while I inspected the damage to my toes, not exactly being able to see much in the dark.

When she answered I asked her what she was doing, and her reply was, 'Sitting on the toilet in the dark.'

I burst out laughing, and when I told her where I was, she laughed with me. I heard her yelling out to Liam and telling him. We laughed and laughed, finding it so absurd. Who knows why, but we did. It reminded me of the little old lady at church the first time we'd gone, and I reminded Patty which made us laugh even more.

'What are you doing tomorrow at lunch?' Patty eventually asked me once we'd calmed down.

'Well, it'll probably be raining again, but hopefully, the electricity will be back on so I'll most likely just stay at the office. You going to come visit me?'

'Yep, I've got something to tell you.'

'Tell me now, you know I'm not going to be able to sleep unless you tell me.'

'No, this is not something I can tell you on the phone, besides it's still a secret.'

'You're pregnant?' I said so loudly that it echoed through the bathroom.

'Goodness, no! There's still more than enough time for babies. I am in no rush, and neither is Liam.'

'Then please tell me, you're cruel!'

Patty just laughed and said she would see me the following day. I had enough of my exam business running around in my head to keep me restless for weeks, and now Patty had just added more fuel to the fire.

Still hobbling, I got myself a glass of orange juice from the fridge and went back to my room. At this moment, I was extremely grateful that I did not live in a huge house. Exhausted still, even after sleeping for practically the whole afternoon, it was not long before I was fast asleep again.

The morning brought with it a dull and overcast day. The rain threatened to drench the already waterlogged lawns just for good measure. As I wobbled on my still sleepy legs to the kitchen, the first thought to enter my mind was strangely enough not whether I would get my results today but about what Patty wanted to tell me. It was so cold, and even the hot shower did not keep my body warm for long.

I left for work with layer upon layer of clothing covering my body, knowing that as the day progressed and the office got warmer from the heater, I would have to de-layer.

The morning dragged by even though I had enough work to keep me busy for days. After two cups of coffee, the same nauseating feeling returned, and I felt congested. I would have to see a doctor soon.

Patty finally arrived at lunchtime, and we sat around the coffee table with hot chocolate and biscuits, keeping warm by the heater.

'So, come on, tell me now.'

'Not many people know this so you can't tell anyone yet, okay?'

'I can't even tell Egan?'

'Oh, you can tell him although I think Liam might have beaten you to it already.'

'Oh come on Patty, tell me already!'

'Well, Liam was approached by Minister Wade two weeks ago with an offer to do missionary work in Lesotho. We didn't want to say anything to anyone – I'm sorry I couldn't tell you – because we wanted to give it to God first. We both felt that if everyone knew about it, our decision might be influenced by people rather than by God.'

Patty stared at me, and I was sure I could detect a well of tears in her eyes.

'I can understand that but you've come to me now, so I forgive you,' I smiled, hoping to ease her tense posture, 'it was probably the right way to go about it. Have you made your decision?'

Patty's lips started to quiver as tears trickled down her cheeks.

I knew the answer. She did not have to confirm it for me.

'When are you leaving?'

'The end of September.'

'That's in a month!' I squealed.

'Do your parents know?'

'We told them last night. My mom was upset at first, understandably, but then they realised it wasn't something we had just decided on a whim and also that it must be what God wants us to do. Dad spoke for a length of time with Minister Wade on the phone and by the end of the evening, they were quite excited for us.'

'Well, it's not like you're moving to the other end of the world. We can still, at least, get to you easily enough.'

'What do you mean? You're moving to Ireland!'

The thought of Patty not living within a few miles' radius suddenly dawned on me.

'Patty, how have our lives changed in the space of a year?'

'Whoever would have imagined it, hey?'

I felt nostalgic, and my heartstrings were pulled watching Patty's face go from sad to happy. We sat silently for a few minutes, both of us thinking our thoughts and considering the latest turn of events.

'I can just see Liam thriving in this kind of work, I'm very sure this is what he has been called to do,' Patty said, wiping away a tear.

I grabbed her hand.

'You too actually. I can picture the two of you building a mission and caring for the children. I don't think there's a vocation in this world better suited for either of you, other than anything that has to do with cars of course.'

We giggled.

'Perhaps we could use cars to create interest with the people there…' Patty trailed off, and I could see her mind filling up with ideas.

And so we came up with one idea after another and speculated as to the living conditions, the people and the weather in Lesotho.

Patty left me, sad that I would be losing my only true friend sooner than expected, but thrilled that she was happy and excited about her and Liam's new venture.

I was about to switch off my computer when finally the email I had been waiting for arrived. Gingerly I opened the email fearing the worst. Glenna stood behind me, and her enthusiasm exploded as she read the email faster than I did.

'Well done, well done!' she shrieked, throwing her arms around my neck.

I just sat and stared at the screen, amazed at the result. I had been awarded 92% for the final practical and my overall mark for the year was 87%. I'd passed with flying colours. I'd never achieved such high grades for any exam in my entire life.

'I can't believe it; I can't believe it. Glenna, thank you. I could never have done it without you. I am so grateful for everything you have done. Thank you!'

I stood up and hugged her so hard. I meant every word from the deepest part of my heart. Glenna rushed out of the office and a few minutes later came back with two glasses and a bottle of sparkling wine.

'We have to celebrate,' she said, popping the bottle open, "it's just sparkling grape juice so you won't have to worry about driving home.'

Right now I didn't mind.

I sent Egan a message and knew our video call tonight would be so exciting as we discussed our future. It would not be long now, and we would be together again. I felt guilty, though, as much as I felt excited. I felt as though I had used Glenna and now that I had what a wanted I was ditching her.

'Glenna, I feel so bad that I am leaving.'

I just had to tell her.

'Nonsense! You have a wonderful future ahead, and whether it is here or in Ireland, I am just happy we got to know each other and that I could help you get there in some small way.'

Tears ran down my cheeks, both from happiness and sadness.

I was a real mixture of emotions when I shared my news with Marco, Josie, Liam and Patty almost immediately when I walked into the Perez's house. It seems they had all known I would pass with flying colours; it was only I that had been doubtful.

When I got home Trey's car was parked in the driveway, as had now become a habit. I chose to delay telling Dena until he'd left or, if he stayed over, it would have to wait until the next day. Surprisingly, though, Dena had heard my car and immediately came rushing over to my cottage to hear if I had received my results yet. When I told her, she exclaimed in a high-pitched voice and gave me a hug from delight. I could not remember the last time or if ever that she had hugged me.

Chapter Twenty-Six

The airport was a gathering ground for unwanted tears. I watched as Liam and Patty made their way through the boarding gates, reminded of Egan's disappearance into thin air. Josie was unable to console herself as she sobbed her goodbyes, burying her face in Marco's arms. Marco too was emotional, and as any loving father would, he had a hard time concealing his tears. December would see them all together again at Christmas in Lesotho, but it was still a way away. It would be the first December ever that I would not be spending Christmas with them.

I spoke to Egan that evening and couldn't let go of the guilt I felt at leaving Glenna.

'I just feel so bad, leaving during the busy season, after all, that she's done for me...'

'That's a natural feeling, and I know we've said a thousand times that you'll come here immediately, but why don't you stay until January, maybe spend Christmas with Dena and then come over?'

Egan's suggestion was what I had wanted to hear from him, but doubt immediately raised its ugly head.

'I don't want to sound paranoid but are you sure you still want me to come over? January is a long way away and, well, I was thinking, well maybe, uh, maybe you don't want me to come over anymore?'

'Vanda,' his voice changed from caring and concerned to stern and authoritative in a split-second, 'have you gone crazy? Do you not have any idea how much I miss you? How much I love you? I'm just thinking about what's best for both of us. If it means being apart for an extra month so we can be happy for the rest of our lives, then so be it. Don't be silly.'

He stared at me through the webcam, and I could see the sincerity in his eyes. I was acting daft and insecure.

'I'm sorry, I know I'm stupid. I love you, and I'm so afraid of something happening that we won't be able to be together.'

'You will love it here. The church here is very similar to the one in South Africa. The people are young and friendly, and

I've even got my sister to come with me. My folks are still adamant about not having anything to do with religion, but they won't push their opinions on Shireen or me.'

I felt so much better by the end of our call. We decided that I would stay with Glenna for the busy season so that I would not feel like I had used and abused her. And I would get to spend one last Christmas with Dena, although this would probably be the first Christmas I actually spent with her. Marco and Josie would be with Liam and Patty in Lesotho. But most of all when I ended the call, I knew that Egan would wait for me forever.

The next morning I took a peek outside my window to see if Dena had any guests. Not seeing any cars parked outside I thought I would go over for a cup of coffee since we had been getting along reasonably well lately. It was a beautiful spring Saturday morning. The birds were filling the trees with nests, all the while chirping and singing and brightening the brisk air. The flowers looked, even more, colourful in the garden under the light clear blue sky.

Wearing just a pair of tracksuit pants, a sweater and my slippers, I opened Dena's kitchen door and went inside. She wasn't in the lounge, and I guessed she was still in bed, so I went back to my cottage. Already quite bored and still somewhat nauseous I went to the pool area with my guitar and sat in the warm sun strumming out the tunes that Egan had taught me - I felt so lonely without him.

After a while, I just lay down in the sun and went back to sleep. A door banged somewhere in the neighbourhood and woke me up. I was hot and sweaty and thought it best to get indoors right away.

I went back to Dena's house entering again through the kitchen door, and this time, I could hear that she was awake. As I entered, I sneezed, and then sneezed a few times more and with it, my nausea increased. The pollen in the air must have been irritating me. My head felt a bit woozy and, rather than land up sick in bed; I went straight to the cupboard in Dena's kitchen where I knew she kept her medicines and took some anti-allergy pills. Dena was still in bed which surprised me as it was most unusual; she never wasted a moment to work. Her bed covered with papers, her laptop and a heap of files, all of them untouched.

'Hello. Are you not feeling well?'

'Does it look like I am feeling well?' she retorted snidely.

'I came here earlier, and you were still sleeping. It's not like you, so that's why I asked.'

'Well, I feel terrible, and I have this proposal to finish by Sunday evening.'

'Can I help in any way?'

'Like you could help me with my work.'

'Sorry, I offered.'

I knew this conversation would lead to a fight and so I left Dena to wallow in her self-pity. She knew where I was if she changed her mind.

Feeling lost, bored and irritated I went to visit Josie. We went to the mall and, just like old times, we walked around all the shops testing perfume and trying out make-up and not buying a thing. I felt happy again and was enjoying the company, so rather than go home and back to that feeling of being alone I stayed there.

It was still such a beautiful day, and we sat outside by the pool reminiscing over the past year. We spoke about the people that had come into our lives and how everything had so drastically changed for the better. Josie spoke about how she missed Patty, and she longed to see her again, but that would only be at Christmas. I understood her pain and her longing as I felt it too.

'When you leave Vanda, what is there here for us?' Marco asked, not expecting an answer, 'I'm going to put the business on the market, there are already a few people interested, and we want to move to Lesotho.'

'Well, I can't blame you for feeling like that. What would you do there, though?'

'When we visit them in December we will have a look around and see what prospects there are for us,' Josie answered, she was confident that it would work out.

We sat outside until the sun set and the night air became chilly. Sometimes we were silent and listened to the still spring air, other times we laughed, or we became sad, but mostly we just enjoyed one another's company. I had long ago spent such quality time with Marco and Josie as today. It was special, and I knew, as did they, that it would be a long time before we spend such time together again.

I made myself comfortable in Patty's bed while I chatted to Egan on my phone. He was as positive as ever of our life together and that Marco and Josie would find a way to be with Patty. He said if he were Marco he would do the same thing. He also said that the fact that Marco would wait until I had left before moving showed how much they loved me as a daughter. I had not quite grasped that thought until Egan had mentioned it. It was only then that I realised how much I would miss them and how much I loved them as my parents. I wondered as I drifted off to sleep whether I would miss Dena.

Minister Wade delivered a sermon that would have softened any heart that held a burden or was hardened. He brought a lump to my throat as he shared a story from his life. His father had taken his life in a state of depression when Minister Wade had been fifteen. He told us how he had searched for answers and got none from his mother who had been so distraught she had shut herself away from her children and the world. He'd felt abandoned and had been full of unanswered questions.

One day to get out of the morbid, dull and lifeless house he went for a walk, and he'd heard singing coming from a church building. He felt it pulling him toward it. He went in and sat at the back of the church, and while the choir sang, he felt that they were singing to him and only to him, calling him to stay, calling him to belong, calling him to serve the One that would give his worried soul all the answers. He stayed for hours after the service had finished, sharing and speaking to the minister and a few other boys his age. That was the first day of his life.

He ended his sermon with, 'God allows everything to happen for a reason, the things you want and the things you don't want. And the Lord is always going to help you through everything, safely and soundly.'

These compelling words I felt were directed solely to me, and that I needed to hear at this very stage in my life. They sunk in deep into my soul, to be stored for when I had to remind myself why things happen as they did in my life.

At home, I found Dena still in bed. She had not touched her work and again I offered to help in any way I could.

'I have not felt this ill in my whole life.'

She was pale and cold to the touch even though she was under a duvet. Perhaps we had the same bug making us feel ill.

'Should I call Dr Preston?'

'No, I'm sure it was that sushi I ate last night. If I'm still not better by tomorrow, then I'll give him a ring.'

'What are you going to do about your work, though?'

'I phoned them and postponed the meeting until next week.'

'Is there anything I can get you or do for you?'

I had never seen her looking like this before, and after Minister Wade's sermon and the fact that she hadn't become the devil in her misery, I felt a heap of compassion for her.

'I think I'll just sleep, I'm sure I'll be fine in the morning.'

Chapter Twenty-Seven

Naturally Glenna was delighted when I told her I would only be leaving after the busy season. This also gave us enough time to find my replacement. The days got increasingly hectic as companies realised it was time to plan their lavish year-end parties and the increase in weddings also began in the spring season.

I had to get to a doctor soon as the feeling of wanting to constantly throw-up would not leave, and the congestion and sneezing had not ceased either.

It had been a few months now since I had seen a car other than Trey's at Dena's house. Of all the men in the world she decided to settle with, it had to be him. In all the time, though, we had still managed to avoid each other, and that suited me just fine.

I dumped the load of files I'd brought home from work on the desk in my study, and as I turned to walk out, my bag caught the edge of a file, and they all came crashing down. Papers fell out and spread all across the floor. Irritated and tired, and not in the least bit amused, I bent down to pick everything up. I forgot about my bag, that was open, as I bent down, all its contents poured out onto the floor on top of the papers. A string of curses expelled from my mouth that I immediately regretted. I straightened up, took a deep breath, told God I was sorry for my bad language, bent down and slowly started picking everything up. Once all the papers were back in the right files, my bag and all its contents safely in my room on the chair, I could relax and rejuvenate in a long hot bubble bath.

Relaxed in my PJs, with a cup of hot chocolate and ready to go through the files and perhaps catch up with some work, I sat at my desk in the study so I could chat to Egan at the same time via a video call -this was not to be. No sooner had I sat down when I heard a door slam shut and a car screeching down the road, tyres spinning as it revved loudly. I presumed that since I had not heard from Dena after checking in on her this morning, she was either feeling better or had got medication from Dr Preston. She had still not been well this morning but had looked much better than the day before. I got up to look out of the window to see if it was Trey that had raced off. Sure enough, it was. So now that had come to an end though it had certainly lasted longer than any other fling she'd had.

She was sitting on the couch, pale, her eyes red and watery.

Has Dena been crying? I never thought I would see the day she cried over a man.

'Hi, you okay?'

I stood in the lounge still holding my cup of hot chocolate not sure what to do. I'd never been in this situation with her before. She looked up at me, a very odd look on her face. I didn't know what to make of her expression at all.

'Was that Trey racing away like a mad thing?'

Dena grunted, 'Oh yeah! He ran like a cat on fire.'

She was not making much sense to me.

'Why? Did you end it or did he?'

'I think you should sit down.'

'Can I get you something before I do? Coffee, tea, juice?'

I wanted to vomit.

'No, please just sit down.'

Dena sounded anxious, almost panicky. I put my cup on the coffee table, sat down on the armchair and lifted my legs up, hugging them to me. She was nervously pulling on the corner of the scatter cushion while she held it close to her chest. She seemed to be fraying at the edges and was simply not herself.

'Did you go to Dr Preston today?' I asked, suddenly realising this might be the cause of her strange behaviour.

Dena nodded her head and bent it down into the cushion. I could not believe what I was seeing.

'So clearly it is not a good diagnosis. Mom, please tell me what is going on!'

I had the feeling that something awful was about to happen. Dena opened her mouth to speak, but no words came out. Instead, she began to sob while holding out a piece of paper for me to read. Both our hands were shaking uncontrollably as I leant over, took it from her and sat back in my chair to read it.

Have I read this correctly?

I read it a few times. My jaw dropped open more and more with every read.

This can't be right.

'WHAT?'

Dena just shook her head.

'WHAT? HOW COULD THIS HAPPEN?' I could not help my yelling. I was horrified at what I had read.

'I mean, I know how, but YOU'RE FIFTY-SIX YEARS OLD!'

'Vanda, I don't know, I don't...' Dena sobbed uncontrollably, not able to finish her sentence.

'How can you be pregnant Mother, how? How?'

And then it suddenly dawned on me why Trey had left so suddenly.

'Trey? You told him?'

'He ran away; won't have anything to do with it.'

My shock moved me to anger.

'He has to. He cannot run away from this. He has to take responsibility. How could you just let him go? It's outrageous.'

'Vanda, I don't know...'

'Mother, this is ludicrous. Were you not careful or did you think it couldn't happen at your age?'

I rambled on, asking one rhetorical question after the other. I just could not wrap my head around this. It was impossible.

'What did you say to Trey? What did he say to you?'

Dena just kept quiet and hugged her cushion.

'When are you going to Dr Preston again?'

'Tomorrow.'

'Well, I am coming with you. I need as much clarity as you do. Oh wait, will Trey be there?'

'Most definitely not.'

'Well, I guess I was not wrong about him then. You better make sure he supports you financially, he is not going to get away with this.'

'I'm not interested in fighting for his support.'

I sat silenced and stunned and far too angry. Dena was going to repeat her past mistakes – another child without a father, born from a mother that had no time for her one child.

'I'm going to get into bed; I'm exhausted.'

Dena stood up and dragged herself to her room. I got up and dragged myself back to my cottage, utterly confused.

What impact would this have on my life?

In bed I phoned Josie. I had to tell her as she would probably walk into a war zone the next morning. Josie was silent on the other end of the phone. She had no words.

I phoned Patty next. She too had no words.

I phoned Glenna and at the same time asked for a few hours off. She had no words except, 'Yes, of course.'

I put my hand on the screen of my laptop trying to ease the tense creases on Egan's face.

'But how?'

He was as shocked and confused as the rest of us.

'Well, I'm sure you know how, the question is, is it even possible?'

'Are you okay love?'

'I don't know yet.' My voice was flat and expressionless.

'Well, I'm sure by January everything will be back to normal and you can still come over here.'

Ireland! I had completely forgotten all about moving to Ireland.

'Oh, Egan! What if it all goes wrong? If I can't get to Ireland what will we do?'

I burst into tears. The impact of what this pregnancy might do to my forever became a daunting reality.

'Let's not get ahead of ourselves. We have to trust God to work it out.'

'Egan, if we can't be together then what's the point of us, of our relationship?'

'It'll work out love, don't doubt God.'

I couldn't think anymore. I would not even comprehend not spending the rest of my life with Egan. Dena and her irresponsible lifestyle were not going to ruin my chance at happiness and my life with Egan.

Chapter Twenty-Eight

Dr Preston's office was stark, cold and unfriendly. The walls adorned with his achievements along with shelves and shelves of books. We sat nervous and sombre in the armchairs in front of his desk, silently waiting for him to take his place on the other side of the desk. He entered the office and quietly closed the door behind him. He was small-boned and short, and I was sure he wore contact lenses in his black eyes that enhanced his head of grey hair.

'Well I'll bet this was a shock,' he said with a grin that neither Dena nor I found amusing at all.

'Okay, I suppose it was not a very pleasant shock.'

'No, not at all in fact,' I made sure he understood my tone of voice.

He told Dena to lie on the consultation bed, and he went through his routine examination. Then Dena redressed and returned to her chair. I was immensely uncomfortable. In the natural process of life our roles in the doctor's room should be reversed, should they not?

'Well you are definitely with child; about six weeks along now. As I said, I'm sure it has been a great shock, but I want to assure you both that even though pregnancies at your age,' and he looked pointedly at Dena, 'are very uncommon, there is no need to be overly concerned. With today's technology, it can be just as easy as the pregnancy of a woman in her twenties.'

I breathed out a sigh of relief as he continued.

'There will obviously be the concern of miscarriage, and you will probably have to stop working sooner than normal. The other concern is your blood pressure. We will have to monitor it very closely so that it doesn't get too high which is a common occurrence in pregnancies of older women.'

Dr Preston chose his words very carefully when he referred to Dena's age. It was a little amusing as he was the only man on earth who knew Dena's real age. Besides my biological father perhaps, but even then I wasn't sure.

'Instead, of monthly checkups, I would prefer to see you every two weeks up to the third trimester and then it will be every week. You must be aware now that you will not carry full-term, and you will have to have a caesarean at about thirty-six weeks.'

He rambled on and on about what might and might not happen. I thought of one thing only – Ireland. I would still be able to go since Dena was not in as much danger as I'd imagined. Dena's complacent attitude was worrisome, though. Would she adhere to the doctor's orders or would she just carry on, as usual, putting her career first, before the welfare of her unborn child?

Josie was waiting to hear all the news in the kitchen when we arrived home. I gave her a brief report of what Dr Preston had told me and she listened with interest.

'Now don't you worry about a thing! I will be here, so you go to Ireland and live your life. I know you are worried, but it will be fine. You can come home when the baby is due, and that will be enough. You can't put your life on hold for this.'

'Are you sure Josie? Won't people think I am selfish and a bad daughter if I leave?'

'The people that know you know of your relationship with Dena and they will understand. The others, well they don't matter now do they?'

Josie always had a way of making sense to me, and as soon as I was back in my cottage I phoned Egan. I could hear the relief in his voice when I explained all that the doctor had said.

'You see love, it will work out fine. Don't stress, rather spend the last few months with Dena in good spirits.'

I knew he was right and told him how much I loved him and missed him.

At work Glenna was very interested in what Dr Preston had told me, asking questions about how they'd control Dena's blood pressure and what medication she would be on. When she was finally satisfied, we could get on with our work as the deadlines remained deadlines regardless even for the sake of our discussions. I was very grateful for the busy schedule at work as it allowed me to forget about Dena and the anger I felt towards her.

Every night I checked in on Dena to make sure she was doing fine. Most nights she got home after I did. As I had suspected, her pregnancy did not seem to slow her down or change her priorities at all. The upside, though, was that there were no more strange cars parked in her driveway.

At Bible study, I told everyone about the situation with Dena, and they too were stunned. They all knew about my relationship with Dena, and as I spoke, Josie held my hand and squeezed it now and then. Tali spoke first, admitting how surprised she was and offering to be available for me should I need someone to talk to or any help. The whole group voiced their support for at least two hours after the Bible study, discussing the pregnancy until it was completely exhausted of all pros and cons.

Dena had still not told her colleagues or her bosses as she claimed that should something go wrong, well, then, at least, no damage was done. She infuriated me with her selfish and callous attitude.

Alice had not been at the previous evening's Bible study, so during a quiet patch at work I phoned her. I wanted to know if Trey was still there or if he had left the country after discovering he was going to be a father.

'He has been in an even worse mood lately, and as you can imagine, the tension is unbelievable. I got that job I told you about closer to home, and I've handed in my resignation. Leaving here cannot come soon enough.'

'Congrats Alice, I'm so happy you can get out of there too, and I'm not surprised he's in a bad mood. He made Dena pregnant,' I said it quickly, and there was an unmistakable silence on the other end of the phone, 'only he won't take any responsibility for it and ran when he got the news. He is the devil.' The anger in my voice appeared once more.

Alice was forced to put down the phone as Trey was walking towards her office, but she came to visit me after work to tell me what had happened after our phone call.

'I waited for several staff members, as well as Mr Drake were within hearing distance then I congratulated Trey on becoming a father. He was so shocked that I knew about it, and Mr Drake was furious that he'd not been the first to know.'

I couldn't help but burst out laughing visualizing Trey's expression.

'Trey exploded in anger, cursed everyone and then some, and stormed off to his office, took his personal belongings and sped off like a maniac.'

Alice shook her head.

'Then Mr Drake called me to his office and accused me of telling lies! So I told him where he could get off and that if Trey was not guilty then why had he run off. Then I told him about how Trey won't acknowledge his part in fathering the child and how his company is the root of all evil. Then I got up and told him I was leaving immediately and not at the end of the month. Naturally Mr Drake went ballistic, but I simply turned around, collected my personal belongings and walked out.'

I wish I'd been a fly on that wall.

Chapter Twenty-Nine

Dena's nausea increased day by day dramatically, along with her bad mood. My nausea had thankfully disappeared completely. She battled to keep anything down, not only in the mornings, the so-called morning sickness lasted just about the whole day. Being the age she was, no one even suspected she was pregnant and just presumed it was menopause. Dena did not correct their thinking either.

It was a week after New Years and the days were getting hotter and, for a few minutes every day after work, I went to my favourite spot on the beach under the tower clock. It was my place of comfort, where I felt close to Egan and especially to God. It reminded me of happier times. Of times when life wasn't so confusing, of times when nothing in life was complicated, and, for a few seconds, I felt like a young girl, madly in love and with friends as young and silly. That afternoon I realised that shortly I would leave home and find another special place in Ireland where I could feel this close to God. Beauty surrounded me that no mortal man would ever be able to create and got home later than usual, the beach and the sunset had been just too inviting to leave.

As I did every night, I went to check on Dena. She had been fine lately, and other than her weight gain, she hadn't changed much. She was lying stretched out on the couch, her legs up on the arm of the couch and her arms crossed over her face.

'Hi, how are you feeling?'

'Awful. My head is pounding; it feels as though it's going to explode.'

'How long have you had this headache?'

'All day and the meeting that went on an entire day didn't help.'

'Why don't you get into bed or have a warm bath and then get into bed?'

'If I move it hurts too much. Even talking to you is hurting.'

When she eventually moved her arms, I could see her cheeks were pale, and I could see the pain she was experiencing in her eyes.

'Have you eaten anything today?'

'Please Vanda, stop talking, and no, I haven't.'

'Get into bed,' I said firmly and helped her up off the couch.

She was weak and unstable as we walked. She climbed very slowly into the bed but had no energy to pull the covers over her. Her room was hot and stuffy, so I opened the window and covered her with a sheet and put a glass of water on the bedside table. Then I switched off the light and went to my cottage and phoned Dr Preston. I explained Dena's symptoms to him, and he seemed highly concerned about what she had eaten and for how long she'd had this headache.

Unlike most doctors, Dr Preston still believed in calling at the patient's home should the occasion arise. He arrived fifteen minutes later and on seeing Dena, he immediately phoned the hospital to tell them to get a bed ready for her. I was horrified; it was just a severe headache.

'Has she been taking it easy?'

'Well I don't know what she's been telling you at her checkups, but she has not changed one single bit. Today she was in a meeting the entire day and had not eaten a thing. She can't keep anything down.'

Dr Preston was furious as he called the ambulance. He explained to me that she was dehydrated and due to the developing child taking up whatever nutrients her body produced, she had nothing left to herself. Her blood pressure had rocketed so high she was in danger of having a stroke - it was far too early in the pregnancy for her blood pressure to be so high. Dena needed to get to the hospital and be re-hydrated urgently. I stood there looking down at her; suddenly she made me so angry again, all she had to do was listen to the doctor's orders but as always, Dena did what Dena wanted to do, regardless of the consequences.

At the hospital, the nurses acted on instructions from Dr Preston and attached several different instruments to Dena. I sat in the waiting room and phoned Josie. I knew they would probably still be on the plane from Lesotho, but I left a message on her phone. I phoned Egan and knew he would be in his Bible study so left him a message too.

People walked by, patients, nursing staff, doctors, cleaning staff; it was an endless flow of movement that, on a normal day would have fascinated me but not today. I watched them mindlessly but could only think of the seriousness of Dena's health. A nurse came to find me and informed me that Dena was now comfortable, and I could see her for fifteen minutes only. She lay in the hospital bed as still as she had been earlier. Machines bleeped around her, interrupting the silence of the room. Dr Preston walked in and closed the door quietly behind him.

'Dena is very fortunate that you phoned. An hour or so longer and she could have suffered a stroke. From now on she will have to stay at home. She will have to work out something with the company she works for, and she is going to have to have a full-time live-in nurse. Both Dena and the baby will be monitored very closely. There's still a long way to go for both of them if they want to come out of this alive.'

'How long will she stay in hospital?'

'When I'm satisfied that her blood pressure is under control then she can go home. But until then she has to stay right here.'

I could sense he was annoyed that Dena had not adhered to his warnings from the beginning. I was livid.

Dr Preston closed the door with a soft click, and I was alone with Dena in the unwelcoming dimly-lit private room. She lay still and straight, covered with the sheet that folded over her now slightly swollen belly, yet she was still very beautiful.

'If you prevent me from going to be with Egan in Ireland, I will never forgive you,' I threatened, knowing she could not hear me or respond.

I was surprised at the level of anger that was welling up inside of me, not only towards Dena and Trey but also towards this unborn child. They all threatened my chance at a lifetime of happiness.

I left Dena and the hospital when Patty phoned me, and I sat in my car in the parking lot repeating all that Dr Preston had said. I also told her how angry I had become. Speaking to Patty made me long to see her again to chat to her face-to-face. This on top of missing Egan and the impact of what Dena's pregnancy might bring, brought about an uncontrollable state of sobs and tears. Patty cried with me, trying to offer words of comfort through her sobs. I would have done just about anything to have Patty next to me, holding me and telling me it would all be fine. We finally ended our conversation amidst tears, sobs and words of love, but I stayed in the car park in my car for a while longer.

Why has this happened? Why has this happened at all?

I silently screamed at the rooftop of the car and sobbed, clutching my face with my hands, the tears streaming through my fingers.

When I got home, Egan finally phoned.

'Please love, don't upset yourself so. If it's not possible for you to come over now, then we will just wait until you can. I will always be waiting for you; you know nothing will change that. I know it's disappointing, but there is nothing we can do about it now. In a few days you will know more, and then we can decide. It's just a little stumbling block; that's all.'

I felt so insecure, and the more Egan tried to reassure me, the more I sobbed, our video call became a one-way conversation. I wanted to reach in through the cyberspace that keeps us apart and touch him, have him hold me and have him take away all my pain.

Chapter Thirty

A slow day at work and a call from Dr Preston aggravated my already overtired and irritated mind. Dena had not improved as much as he had hoped after four days, and she would have to stay in the hospital for a few more days. The support I received from everyone at church was simply amazing. Phone calls, text messages and simple hugs were comforting, and I welcomed each and every one. But all this love and support did not abate the anger that flowed through me like a tidal wave on a daily basis.

What has happened to the carefree and relatively happy person I've been my entire life?

Will this anger ever subside?

Will I ever be able to forgive Dena for upsetting my plans for the future?

Will I ever accept this child?

And so on and so on I pondered these questions. I couldn't remember the last time I had laughed.

Alice phoned as I arrived home to tell me she had heard from an ex-colleague at Luxous that Trey had left the country and was in Asia somewhere. Was it possible that my anger could get any worse? Yes, it was.

I went to Josie and Marco and ranted about how Trey had just run away and left me with this mess. Why should he be able to get away with it?

'There is nothing you can do about it and besides, do you want to have him in your life?' Josie asked softly and gently.

'No, I don't want him in my life but he could, at least, accept some responsibility and help financially.'

'Do you need financial help?'

'No, but it's the principal of the matter.'

'Vanda, listen to what you're saying. You don't want him in your life, and if he were to help you financially, then he would be. It's better this way.'

'It is not right to be this angry, Vanda. God would not want you to feel this way, so it's then better not to have the people around that make you feel like this,' Marco added.

'In that case, Dena and that child should not be in my life either.'

Josie, who was standing next to me, put her arms around me and hugged me lovingly.

'My dear child, if I could take this away from you I would, but I can't and so don't be angry, we are all here to help you. But most of all you must not shun God by being so angry. Somewhere in all this upset, He has a plan for you. You have to believe He will show it to you, just be patient, please.'

Josie was almost begging, and I could hear the lump in her throat thickening her words.

'I know, it's just so hard to accept it all.'

I left, still feeling like I wanted to punch the next person I saw, and took a drive to the tower clock. It was dark, so I sat in the car with the window down and let the smell of the sea breeze consume me. It was all I could do to release this unusual and uncontrollable anger I had developed.

After a week in the hospital, Dena was finally allowed to go home. She was not however allowed to return to work. Derrick Callier and a few other senior directors came over to the house at my request to discuss Dena's future within the firm. As she was not merely an employee but a director and a member of the Board, they were eager for her to regain her health and return to work. Their initial response to the news that she was in fact not suffering from menopause but from pregnancy was laughable even if it was not a joke. Needless to say, it provided for a lot of gossip at the firm once the news had spread. We decided that she would work from home and that they would keep her workload to a minimum. Dena, of course, tried her best to convince everyone that she was fine and would cope. She tried to state her case once too often, and I exploded, yelling at her to stop being so selfish and had she not been irresponsible enough for a lifetime.

'Who do you think you are talking to?' she asked when I finally finished screaming.

'I'm talking to you, stupid irresponsible you! You think that the world revolves around you, and you can just carry on as if there is nothing wrong! Well, I have news for you! You are fifty-six and pregnant, get that into your stupid head!'

I stormed out of the room in tears and went back to my cottage, leaving poor Derrick to convince Dena that I was indeed correct.

Josie walked into the cottage sheepishly about an hour later. I was lying on the couch, tears of anger staining my cheeks.

'Wow. I've heard the two of you argue before, but I've never heard you speak to her like that.'

'I don't care anymore, Josie.'

'Vanda, don't say that. As much as she's upset you and she is very wrong, she needs you. She needs all of us; she just doesn't realise it yet, she is too selfish, always has been.'

'I don't want to talk about her.'

'Okay, but just to let you know she has agreed to work from home, and Derrick told me when he was leaving that he had not realised the seriousness of the situation, and he will be sending very little work, if any, to Dena.'

'Well thank goodness for small mercies.'

Josie left, and I could see she was anxious about both Dena and me. I felt bad that I'd been rude to her; she was only kind and loving to me as she always was. I wanted to sleep off my anger first, and then I would go over to her house with a peace offering – her favourite peppermint chocolate.

The familiar sound of a video call ringing through my laptop woke me up earlier than expected, not that I minded. Greeted by the beautiful Irish smile of my forever.

'Hello love, how are you?'

'I'm fine and you?' I lied.

He smiled endearingly, and I knew he was missing me as much as I was missing him.

'How is Dena doing?'

I told him of the day's events and how angry I was and how even Josie had been shocked at my behaviour.

'I don't like being this person that is so angry all the time, but I get so mad the minute I start to think of Dena.'

'Just think that in a short while you'll be here, and let that calm you down.'

'It can't happen soon enough.'

Egan's constant positive attitude made my heart pound. The Dena situation would have given any person a reason or an excuse to end a relationship, but he held on tightly, knowing and trusting that God would show the way for us to be together. If I could just adopt the same faith, I would probably be able to deal with my anger a lot better.

After church on a hot and humid Sunday morning, while we had refreshing juice instead of the usual tea and coffee, Minister Wade stood beside me and whispered, 'Don't leave, I want to speak with you when everyone has left if you've got the time.'

'Sure,' I said, my voice sounded surprised and questioning.

We sat on the steps at the back entrance to the church building.

'I like to sit here; it somehow makes things a little less tense and impersonal.'

I didn't agree or disagree and let him continue.

'How is your mom doing?'

I sighed.

Was this really what he wanted to talk to me about?

I had calmed down and enjoyed the service so much, now did I have to talk about Dena and let all that anger lift itself from within my bodied dimness?

'I know this is so difficult, you and Egan had plans, and now they've all been put on hold. It understandable you're angry.'

'Is it that obvious?'

'You can't help it. I just want you to know that whenever you want to talk or cry or scream I'm here for you. Your friends here at church are here for you. God is here for you Vanda, He always is.'

'Can I punch you?' I said in a half serious, half joking tone.

Minister Wade just smiled.

'It's just like....'

The tears rolled down my cheeks, and I battled to keep my feelings in check.

'I don't want to be this angry person. Dena and I have always had a difficult relationship and now I'm supposed to support her unconditionally when she has ruined my chance of being with Egan in Ireland.'

I took a deep breath to replace my natural instinct to be angry, 'I just don't know what God wants from me, and that frustrates me too.'

'Do you believe that Egan will wait for you, wait until after the birth of Dena's baby?'

'Yes, he has said so on many occasions. I just find it difficult to believe.'

'If you leave now, and something goes critically wrong with Dena or the baby, will you be able to forgive yourself?'

'I have not thought about that. I only thought that I could go to Ireland and come back for the birth.'

'If you wait for six months then when you do go it will be forever, and you won't have to worry about coming back or being on standby for a phone call.'

I thought carefully about what he said.

'I know you're right. I must just get my brain to believe it.'

'Like I said before, don't cut us off, we're all here for you and most of all let God help you. He knows best.'

Minister Wade held my hand while we prayed and I felt a sense of calm come over me, and I felt at peace. I knew that I had to take control of my anger and not let it control me. Egan and I would be together one day and then it would be forever, it might just take a little longer than I'd planned.

And what are a few more months in the greater scheme of things?

Chapter Thirty-One

The baby's growth was slow and slightly behind what doctors deemed normal, but Dr Preston was not too concerned about it. It was fascinating to see Dena's belly increase and transform into the shape of a ball. As the weeks went by it became amusing to watch Dena's disdain at her gained weight. Dr Preston was more concerned with Dena's fluctuating high blood pressure, which, as the pregnancy progressed, fluctuated more and more. My nausea had stopped though her appetite had not returned, and Dena remained either on the couch or in bed, moving around as little as possible. I had moved from my cottage into my old bedroom in Dena's house so that I could be nearer to her in the evenings and the early mornings before Josie arrived. Dr Preston had requested that it was either this or we had to employ a full-time nurse. It was a strange feeling, moving back into my old bedroom. Not the feeling of returning to a happy place but more like moving into a room I'd always wanted to leave.

Egan remained constant in his belief that we would be together once the baby was born and his family was eagerly awaiting my arrival in Ireland. I found that once I gained control over my anger towards Dena and the baby I could cope with helping her, and I felt more like the person I knew I was. There were still times when I wanted to slap Dena so hard – I even threw a cushion at her one day – but I managed to pull myself together. Rather than explode and say things I knew I would regret, I would walk away or take a drive to the beach and sit by the tower clock to calm down.

The nights we had Bible study were the best nights of the week. After study everyone always wanted to hear the progress on Dena and it was a relief to talk and get everything off my chest.

I had several more conversations with Minister Wade on the back steps and often his wife Jackie joined us, sharing what it was like to be pregnant and the changes one's body went through.

On an overcast autumn day, I walked into the living room after church. Dena was lying on the couch like she usually did, and where I'd expected to find her. She had her arm over her eyes shading her face from the light; her other arm hanging off the couch, fingers dangling on the floor.

'Hi Mom, how are you feeling?'

Dena did not answer, and I thought she was sleeping. A feeling of unease washed over me and instinct moved me to check on her more closely. I threw my bag onto the coffee table as I grabbed her arm.

I shook her by the shoulders and took her other arm off her face. Her eyes flickered, and she moaned, 'Phone doctor...'

That was all she said, and it was all I needed to hear. I snatched my phone from my bag and dialled Dr Preston, and then the ambulance, then Josie. Dena was moaning, not able to produce any clear words.

'Mom is your head sore or are you having pains from the baby?'

'Head...'

I knew her blood pressure had peaked again. That bleak look on her cheeks and the anguished frown on her face clearly indicated she was in pain.

I sat in the waiting room while Dr Preston and the nursing staff worked as fast as was humanly possible. Everyone knew Dena from her numerous visits to the hospital, and everyone was willing to assist swiftly. But this time, it was different. Her blood pressure was so high by the time she reached the hospital that she had suffered a mild stroke. The baby was under a lot of stress, and they were both in danger of losing their lives.

I sat and prayed and held my breath every time the door opened expecting to see Dr Preston coming to deliver bad news.

Not long after Josie and Marco arrived to be with me, Minister Wade also arrived. We held hands while Minister Wade prayed that God would spare them but that it would be His will and not ours and that I would have the strength to accept His will. My legs were shaking, and my hands were trembling, and I was sweaty all over as we waited for what seemed like hours in the cold white waiting room. Eventually, even the cushioned chairs became uncomfortable.

Dr Preston finally walked into the room, and my heart sank. I knew from the look on his face that it was not good news.

Can I handle bad news? No, I can't. It can't be bad news. It can't be.

'Vanda my dear, I would like to speak to you alone, please.'

'No, please, I would rather they be here.' I looked at Josie next to me, and she gave me a reassuring smile.

He sat down in the armchair next to me.

'Dena's blood pressure was so high that since she'd been admitted, she's suffered another stroke.'

I gasped.

'She has developed preeclampsia that is very dangerous at this stage in her pregnancy and if we can't get her blood pressure down she could go into a coma and the baby might also not survive.'

My head was spinning as I tried to make sense of what he was saying.

'What is pree...?'

'Preeclampsia is a condition a woman develops during pregnancy if her blood pressure is not kept under control. There are several things that could potentially happen, but I'd rather refer you to literature than have you sit here while I explain, as I'm sure you won't remember any of it by the time I leave the room.'

Josie squeezed my hand. I felt the blood draining from my face and rush into the pit of my stomach stirring my nerves into a crazed frenzy.

'What we have to be most concerned about at this time is to get her blood pressure under control; her body seems to be rejecting everything we try.'

I gasped again.

'Can I see her?'

'In a little while, the nurse will come and fetch you.'

Dr Preston left, and I sat numb and confused, frozen in my chair. The others were silent too, just as stunned as I was. A nurse old enough to be my grandmother walked into the room and with the sweetest voice told me I could see Dena. I lifted myself up onto my shaky legs and while holding on to Josie we walked slowly to Dena's room. She hugged me at the door and suddenly I was alone. Hesitantly I entered the room that, except for the sound of the machines, was silent, with death looming in the shadows. I sat next to her bed. She was still and straight, and the machines bleeped and buzzed around us. I held her hand as it rested on the bed and stared at her, willing her to get better for her sake as well as for the sake of the baby.

'Hi Mom,' I said, 'come on Mom, wake up, please get better.'

I bent my head and rested it on the edge of the bed and while I prayed I cried, begging her to get better. She lay there like a corpse.

'Mom please, please, I'm sorry we never got along but please, please get better.'

My shoulders shook as I sobbed uncontrollably, gripping her hand tightly as the sound of the machines accompanied the sound of my unhappiness.

A tap on my shoulder woke me up an hour later, my head still resting on the bed and my hand still in Dena's.

'Would you like us to arrange a bed for you here in the room?'

It was the same sweet lady who asked me as she checked the machines and made sure they were still bleeping out the correct rhythms.

'Thank you that would be very kind of you.'

I went to the coffee shop to get a dose of caffeine and a blueberry muffin while the extra bed was being set up. I phoned Egan and gave him an update on Dena and, like always, he remained devoted to our reunion sometime in the near future.

Before returning to the room, I went to the bathroom and took my time freshening up. I stared in the mirror at my face and my tired swollen eyes, not ever imagining the mayhem to which I would return – a flurry of nurses acting swiftly under the instructions of Dr Preston.

'What's going on?' My heart skipped a beat.

'Vanda my dear, you should not be in here right now, please will you wait in the waiting room? I will be there shortly.'

I turned around and walked to the waiting room like a zombie. I sat down on a chair and just stared at the floor. Josie, Marco and Minister Wade had left; I was alone, alone to face what I feared most.

What is he going to tell me next? What precl...disease will he tell me she has now?

A while later Dr Preston walked in and spoke to me softly.

'That was a little scary now wasn't it? I'm sorry I chased you off like that. Dena's blood pressure went a bit crazy there for a while, but we managed to get it back under control.'

'Can I see her again now?'

'Yes, yes please do.'

I breathed out a sigh of relief. It was not what I had feared, and perhaps Dena would survive this, I tried to convince myself rather unconvincingly.

Again, she was as still as a corpse as I sat next to her holding her hand. The baby moved or kicked; I wasn't sure what they called it. The sheet shook as the baby kicked again and, as I rested my hand on Dena's belly, it kicked once more. I jerked my hand away, amazed at what I had felt and quickly put my hand back waiting and hoping it would happen again. I guess the baby decided that was enough entertainment for the night as I never felt it move again. I phoned Josie. I had to tell someone.

'Josie, guess what happened? I felt the baby move! It kicked my hand! It was the weirdest feeling.'

Josie just laughed and explained that it was normal and that it meant the baby was healthy and alive.

Since the baby was not going to keep me company I decided to go home to my cottage and get some much needed silent, peaceful rest. Sleeping in the bed next to Dena was not, I figured, perhaps such a good idea after all.

Chapter Thirty-Two

There is nothing like one's bed to achieve complete and much-needed rest. I allowed the covers and the mattress to swallow me as I sunk into a deep, sound, calm sleep. For about three hours.

My phone rang so loudly that I sat up straight like a pole, the covers flying right off the bed and in one movement I had the phone by my ear.

'Hello?' I answered, wide awake.

'Vanda, this is Sister Weir from the hospital. I apologise for waking you at this hour, but Dr Preston asks if you would please come down to the hospital immediately.'

'What's going on?'

'I'm sorry, I can't say. Please come as soon as you can.'

'Uhm, okay. Thank you for phoning. Tell Dr Preston I will be there soon.'

I sat for a few seconds stunned, the phone still in my hand.

Was Dena alive?

Had her blood pressure gone out of control again and did she have that preecalm thing?

After pulling on a pair of jeans, a loose sweater and sneakers, I thought of phoning Josie and asking her to go with me. Then I reconsidered it as Josie needed the rest too and there would not be anything she could do whatever the situation.

The city streets were quiet and dark, encouraging me to speed and I only yielded at the stop streets and traffic lights, not wanting to waste a second.

The hospital corridors seemed longer than usual as I ran towards Dena's room. When I finally reached it, I could not help the eerie feeling that attacked me at the doorway, a feeling that something had gone horribly wrong. A nurse was standing beside the bed fiddling with a new machine with a different bleep. Dena's skeletal body lay on the bed inflated at the abdomen by the baby.

'I'm Vanda, Dr Preston told me to come in,' I stuttered breathlessly.

'Please wait here, I will fetch Dr Preston.'

She disappeared from the room, and I stood there looking around at the machines and the space where the bed for me had been. Dr Preston rushed in.

'Thank you for coming Vanda, please sit down.'

He motioned to the armchair next to Dena's bed as he leaned against the bed, crossed his arms over his chest and looked at me. I could see he was choosing his words wisely.

'I'm afraid your mother has made a turn for the worst. Not long after you left, her blood pressure shot up so high that she started having seizures, it's what we call eclampsia.'

'What?'

'It's the term used when seizures occur from severe preeclampsia. In other words, your mother, Dena's condition has reached a critical stage. The seizures have put her life and that of the baby in severe danger. Every time she has a seizure the oxygen supply gets lessened to the baby. It is a very, very serious situation.'

'When I left here, she was calm, and everything was under control. How did all this happen?'

'It is a very unpredictable condition that she has, but I'm afraid that from here on she will not recover.'

I quivered at his words.

'What do you mean, not recover?'

My voice went up an octave.

'What I mean, Vanda is that we can keep Dena alive on machines for another week for the sake of the baby, and then we will have to do a caesarean and deliver the baby.'

My mouth hung open, and I felt my heart race at a thousand beats a second. My breaths were short and shallow as I started to gasp, trying to get a grip on the reality I had just got dealt. My skin went cold and sweaty, and I could feel the blood drain from my face. I wanted to speak, but no words released from my brain. My stomach felt hollow, and the nerves took over as my body began to shake. I heard Dr Preston calling out to the nurse who rushed off and returned with water and a pill and, with some effort, managed to get me to swallow it.

What is happening? What is happening? I kept asking myself over and over again in my state of panic.

'Vanda, please breathe, breathe my girl.'

'She is going to die when the baby is born?' I asked in a small voice, not wanting his answer.

'I'm sorry Vanda, but it's almost definite that either Dena or the baby will not make it and if Dena does make it she will remain in a coma.'

'NO NO NO NO NO it can't be! This cannot happen!'

Dr Preston put his hand on my shoulder in a gesture of compassion. I jumped up and moved away from him, away from the bed, away from the death.

'YOU SAID IT WOULD BE FINE; YOU SAID A LOT OF WOMEN HER AGE HAVE BABIES! YOU SAID IT WOULD BE FINE!'

Trembling, I tried to grab something and then it went dark. It felt like I was floating and then something hard touched my back and I heard voices and felt movements around me.

'Vanda, Vanda can you hear me? Vanda?'

My eyes flickered open to the faces of Dr Preston and the sweet old nurse hovering over me.

'Hello again dear, you fainted dear. We lifted you onto a bed in the next room. Just lie here for a while, we will be here with you.'

'Is there someone we can phone for you?' the sweet old nurse asked.

'Josie please.' I mumbled, giving them my phone from my pants' pocket.

'I'm so sorry that this has happened Vanda; I could make it better if Dena's body were willing.'

I put my hand over my eyes as the sobs seeped from my shuddering chest. I tried not to think about what had happened, all that was said and what was in store for me now.

'How is the baby?' I squeaked finally, once the sobs had subsided.

'She is doing remarkably well at the moment. She is under a lot of stress, but she has a good heartbeat. She's a fighter. I think she will be just fine.'

I was about to scold Dr Preston for the time he'd said that Dena would be fine when now she was anything but fine, but suddenly I realised what he had just said.

'She? The baby is a girl?'

'Oh, yes, sorry I thought you knew. Yes, it's a girl.'

I tried to wrap my mind around the idea of the baby in Dena's tummy being a girl. I couldn't. I couldn't think of the baby as anything other than an it. I was able to sit up without feeling woozy with the help of the sweet old nurse, who had a glass of water ready for me to drink.

'Sometime very soon we need to discuss the baby,' Dr Preston said quietly.

'What do you mean?'

'Are you going to raise the child yourself or do you want to give it up for adoption?'

I felt woozy again.

'Me? What do I know about a baby?'

It was all just too much to digest right then and there. The anger I had managed to control for so long flew out of me with a vengeance when I realised I would never get to Ireland and Egan.

'I DON'T WANT THE BABY! WHY MUST I HAVE THE BABY? IT'S NOT MY BABY!'

'No decision is necessary at this very moment; we will talk about it again tomorrow when things are calmer.'

'Vanda.'

I was so relieved to hear Josie's voice I burst into fresh tears.

'Oh, Josie! It's not fair!' I cried as she rushed to my side and held me in her arms, still unaware of the severity of the situation.

I clung to her tightly, as if in doing so she could erase all the horrible chaos. Josie held me and rubbed my arms and back, my tears and sobs slowly ebbing away.

'What is going on?' she asked Dr Preston

He explained the events of the last few hours while I held onto her tightly, shutting out his words not wanting to hear them again. I felt Josie jerk and her head bent down to my neck. She had heard.

'Oh Vanda, I am so sorry.'

She cried with me, and I cried with her. Carefully she released her hold on me enough to phone Marco with the news, sobbing all the while.

'Marco will be here soon,' she said to me brushing my hair lovingly from my face.

I looked at her with my flushed cheeks and red swollen eyes.

'What must I do with the baby?'

'Shoo, let's wait until Marco gets here and we can all discuss it then okay?'

Why would God give me such a burden?

The sweet old nurse went to order us coffee and Dr Preston went to check on Dena; it was just Josie and me left in the room.

'I can't help but be so angry. I know Minister Wade helped me through the anger, but it seems to have all come back now. Why must I have the baby? What do I know about a baby?'

Marco rushed into the room, and I am sure Josie was relieved that she did not have to answer my questions. Behind Marco, to my surprise, was Minister Wade. A rush of relief washed through me now that they were both there. Maybe, just maybe, sanity would prevail. We held each other while my tears kept falling and for all the words of comfort that we uttered, all I wanted to do was -scream.

Dr Preston returned to the room and explained the situation to everyone once more, and again I found it difficult to accept the obvious outcome. We bowed our heads while Minister Wade prayed for Dena and the baby's health and for Josie and Marco and me to reach out to Him for the strength we would need in the days to come. I felt exhausted, and it was an effort to open my eyes when Minister Wade had finished praying. Dr Preston gently suggested we all go home as there was nothing more to do except wait. We would discuss the baby's future when we could think more rationally.

Chapter Thirty-Three

After a telephone call with Glenna where I explained what had happened, I made coffee, got back into bed and phoned Egan. I knew he would be at work, but I had to tell him and I needed to know how the baby would affect our relationship. I couldn't stand the never-ending scenarios and assumptions playing games with my mind.

'Hello my love,' he answered.

His Irish accent was becoming increasingly thicker the longer he was in Ireland. As always he was cheerful and his voice full of positives.

Would this be the last time we spoke?

I was silent, trying to find the right words to tell him.

'Vanda, what's wrong? What's happened with Dena and the baby?'

I heard him excusing himself from the office and a door closed behind him.

'Vanda, please tell me what's going on!'

I thought there were no more tears left in me and yet they rolled down my face, a lump and sobs choking my throat.

'Dena, in a coma…baby okay…' I managed to utter.

'Oh! My love! I am so sorry. What do the doctors say?'

I took an extremely deep breath, forcing enough oxygen into my lungs so that I could explain what had happened. After relating my version of the past evening's events, I waited for his response.

'You have to take the baby Vanda; it's still your blood, and it is what is right.'

'I know it is, but I'm just so angry that this is now my responsibility. I just can't understand what God is planning for me with a baby that is not even mine. It's confusing, and it just makes me so angry.'

As I spoke, I could feel the anger towards Dena boiling through my veins. Her life was a ride of selfishness and her lifestyle of male visitors had ultimately cost her, her life and yet it was I that had to live with the consequences. I wanted to go to the hospital and pummel her still almost lifeless body just at the thought of it.

'Don't try to work out what God's plan is for you. It will all get revealed to you at some stage. I know it's easy for me to talk here, thousands of miles away, but you must trust God to get you through this His way. Have you spoken to Minister Wade?'

'Yes, he came to the hospital with Marco last night. I wasn't exactly pleasant, and with so many questions and the exhaustion, it was not a good time to speak to him.'

I took another very deep gulp of air.

'What about us?'

'What do mean? What about us?' he asked, sounding shocked.

'Well, I won't be able to come to Ireland as soon as we planned, and it is already a year later than we originally planned! And now I have a baby to take care of, and that's for a lifetime...' I trailed off.

'I still don't understand what the issue is.'

'Egan, it's not just me anymore, there's a baby. Are you willing to raise a baby that's not yours? What do we know about babies?'

'The baby will be yours, and you're all I want. I have parents that will help.'

Somehow God led this Irish lad into my life and for that, I was forever grateful.

The sobs and tears found their way back to my throat as I became overwhelmed with relief and gratitude, and I cried over the phone as Egan tried and tried to comfort me through his tears.

'Vanda, my love, my life is with you, forever. If it comes with a package, that's okay, as long as you're with me. If it takes us another six months or another year to be together, it doesn't matter. We will have forever to make up for it.'

'I love you,' were the only words I could manage and the only ones that mattered.

We spent nearly an hour on the phone even though he was supposed to be working. He said once they heard the situation they would be sympathetic. I could only hope so.

I'd just ended the call with Egan when Patty phoned. Josie had phoned her to tell her the news and once again I was hit by how much I missed her. After listening to me ramble on for ages about the baby and Dena and Egan, Patty finally had the chance to tell me her news. They were on their way to a remote village for a couple of months and would not be anywhere near a phone or any communication. She knew the timing was not the best and even suggested they postpone their trip. It took me ages to convince her that there was nothing she could do to change the inevitable and that Dena should not be the reason they too changed their lives. After I had ended the call, I felt so alone. My best friend and my partner were both miles and miles away. What would I do if Josie and Marco were not around, and if Glenna was not so understanding, or if I did not have a support group in my friends from church? I had to realise that I was not alone at all.

The next call was to the hospital. A different nurse spoke to me and confirmed that there was no change. Then I phoned Josie. If I were going to raise this child, I would probably need things, and since Dena had not bothered buying anything yet, there was still nothing for the baby. Josie was delighted with the prospect of shopping. It was perhaps just what I needed to begin thinking of raising a child.

Going to the mall brought back the all too familiar feeling of days when I was much younger and Josie, and I would spend a day walking in and out of shops having as much coffee at as many coffee shops as possible, to pass the time while Marco and Patty worked on their cars. I dared to think that the shopping we would be doing today would be very different, but thankfully the coffee shops would still be the same.

After deciding on a time to meet, I had a refreshing shower, feeling as though I was washing all the horror of the previous evening away. I felt more confident in the challenge of keeping the baby after my phone call with Egan, the fear of resenting the baby for ruining my forever with Egan eliminated, and it was possible that this was the reason I felt more at ease with the idea of a baby. As I walked from the bedroom to the kitchen with a clean body, fresh hair and wearing a pair of jeans, a blue sweater and pumps, I looked about the cottage.

Would the cottage be big and safe enough to raise a child in, or would I have to move into the house? I did not like the house at all.

Josie was ready and waiting with a list almost two pages long of things we had to buy.

'It's just a baby, what on earth do we need so much stuff for?' I glanced through the list, not recognising half the items listed.

On our way to the mall, I raised the subject of the cottage versus the house.

'For the first month perhaps you should move in with us. At least, then we can help you, and the baby adapt.'

'Uhm, actually I hadn't even thought of that. Oh Josie, how am I going to manage this? I haven't got a clue have I?'

'It's going to be very difficult in the beginning, but I'm sure, no, I know, you will be just fine.'

'What if I don't like the baby? What if I just can't get the hang of this baby business and what if the baby doesn't like me?'

'Now you're letting your mind run away with you. Just relax and let's buy all these goodies first, and when the baby is born then you deal with all those fears with us together, okay?'

'Thank you, Josie, you know I love you. As always, you are the one that I can rely on, what would I do without you?'

Although Josie simply fobbed me off, I knew that she knew how grateful I was and how much I loved her as my mother.

We stood in one of the many baby shops in the mall in complete awe of the many choices on offer. How were we to make a decision, and the right one at that? Josie was fascinated by the varieties and kept remarking how in her day there had been a choice of perhaps one or two different varieties of prams and cots, but today it was like walking into a candy store.

I was relieved to find Tali in the same store we were in and, without hesitation I went over to her pulling Josie with me and pleaded for her help. Tali smiled in amusement at our blatant lack of knowledge of the matters of baby components. She explained the pros and cons of the items that Josie and I were interested in, and after a while, she'd forgotten what she had originally come to buy as she delved into our long list.

At the checkout point, I looked at the heap of purchased items, at Josie and Tali and then back at the items.

'Is all this stuff necessary? I can understand the cot and pram and nappies and perhaps also clothes, but all this other stuff? It's only going to be a small baby...' I trailed off.

'A month after the baby is born you will be buying more things,' Tali grinned, to my astonishment.

I felt sickened and depressed; this was so permanent. I needed to talk to Tali a bit more and invited her to join us for coffee. While munching on a quiche, which I was sure was tasty and yet my downcast mood allowed it not to be, Tali asked, 'Have you got a name for the baby?'

Josie and I looked at each other, both thinking the same thing. No, we did not. It had not even crossed my mind that the baby would need a name. Tali had a giggle and promised to lend me her book of baby names. Josh, Tali and Coco were eagerly awaiting the birth of their son and brother. I got easily drawn to Tali; she had a passion that one could not refuse to notice. Secretly I thanked God that Tali had been in the same store at the same time. I'm sure God just laughed at me and said, "You're welcome, my child.'

Chapter Thirty-Four

I woke up and was progressively more anxious than the previous day, as the end of the week drew near. I knew what was waiting for me but that final day, time, the moment had not yet been confirmed. It left a gnawing feeling in my stomach just at the thought of what was going to happen – that final outcome, the sorrow, the fear and the uncertain future. Every time my phone rang my heart sank and began beating at a pace so fast it was difficult to breathe. And each time I had to calm myself before answering with shaking hands.

Glenna, being the incredible person that she was, understood the emotional roller coaster I was riding and allowed me the time off work to stay at the hospital. If there was any emergency she couldn't handle, she promised to call me. She had also insisted that I take a month off when the baby arrived, like any other mother on maternity leave.

To compound my already anxious state of mind, I could not help but worry that one day soon, Egan would finally realise what his commitment entailed. Then he would decide that it was all too much for him, and that would be my forever, gone forever. I was on this constant emotional high and low as every second beat along.

Dr Preston was waiting for me when I arrived at about midday at Dena's hospital room. There seemed to be a hum of activity, but it did not seem to be urgent or critical. The hum did not bode well for me, though, as I slowly and quietly made my way to the chair next to Dena's bed. I just knew what Dr Preston wanted to tell me.

'Would you prefer to talk in my office or are you fine here?'

'Here, please. When?'

'Tomorrow morning, eleven o'clock.'

I took a gulp of air and turned to look at Dena's lifeless body, still commandingly beautiful even in its comatose state. Her belly was large and round, and protruding awkwardly.

'We will take her off the machines as soon as the baby is safely out. I don't want to concern you now about the procedure; that can wait until just before we go into theatre.'

'Thank you. Can I have someone with me or must I be on my own?'

'Usually, in childbirth only the spouse is allowed in, but since this is not a normal situation you may ask one other person to be with you.'

'Thank you.'

I chose not to say anything further for fear that the anger still hovering within me would unleash itself. Dr Preston patted me on my shoulders in a kind and comforting way, but I was not comforted at all. Soon after he left, all the nursing staff left as well, closing the door behind them, leaving me alone with Dena. For a while I just sat, motionless and dumbstruck, not able to think of anything, listening to the silence and the machines bleeping. So the time had come. I knew the time had been steadily approaching but still I felt numb and wished, oh how I wished, that the burden disappears from me. I sat frozen in the chair.

Am I ready for the future?

Definitely not, but there was nothing I could do to change it. Nothing at all. That was how I spent the next two hours, sitting in the chair numb, frozen and so afraid of the future. The only way I would get through the evening would be at Josie's house. Patty's room was generously converted into a room for me, with enough space for the baby and all its necessities.

First I went home to my cottage to make sure I had taken everything over that I would need for the next few weeks.

'Hello, my love,' Egan's upbeat voice with its thick Irish accent always lifted my spirits, even now, mostly now, during this depressive and anxious time.

I needed him so much.

'It's time. Tomorrow morning at eleven o'clock Dr Preston will deliver the baby and then switch off the machines.'

As I spoke, the tears raced down my cheeks, sobs escaping like a jackhammer from my throat and there was nothing I could do to prevent it. I put my head down on the kitchen counter and cried and cried and cried, not hearing Egan trying his utmost to console and ease my burdened heart.

'I wish you were here. What am I going to with a child? I'm so scared,' I said through the never-ending train of tears.

'Vanda, my love, I wish I could leave here now and be with you. But you know how tightly the contract binds me. This timing is so bad, I want to be with you; you must know that my love.'

The tears poured down my face, wetting the counter as they dripped off my chin.

'I'm so sorry about your mother, my love. I have no words that could help make sense of it all right now. Hold onto God is all I can say, and say goodbye to her before the machines are switched off. I will be with you in spirit; you must know that my love.'

'How do I say goodbye? How?'

'You will know when it's time. Ask God to give you the right mind and words and, when you do, it will be over. There won't be any more guessing or any more waiting, and no more suffering.'

It was hopeless trying to speak to him or even to try and listen to his wise words, all I wanted to do was cry, sob and yell at the walls asking them, 'WHY? WHY? WHY?'

Ending the video call with the promise to call back later from Josie's, I dumped the last of my things into my car and put on my thick, woollen camping jacket as the night air had taken a sudden turn towards freezing. Then I took a last look around inside and left the cottage.

Egan had phoned Josie, concerned about my current state of mind, so by the time I reached the house, she had a hot bath running with lavender oils and salts and a glass of red wine waiting. The water eased through my body as I slowly submerged myself in the tub. The water tipped over the edge of the bath and trickled onto the floor as I sank beneath the warm, soothing water. Josie sat on the little stool next to the bath and waited until I had soaked in the oils for a few minutes before speaking.

'Marco asked Minister Wade to come over, do you mind?'

'That's fine, thanks.'

I soaked a little longer before speaking again. The room had by now completely misted up from the steam.

'Dr Preston said that because it is such an unusual situation I can have someone with me during the delivery of the baby. You feel up to it Josie, please?'

The usual flow of tears blended in with the bath water on my face. Josie did not bother to subdue her sadness or tears - this was just as emotional a time for her as it was for me.

'Of course, I will. Marco and Minister Wade said they would be there outside the door praying.'

Her lips trembled as she spoke and she stroked a few strands of hair away from my face.

'Egan phoned me. He is so worried about you and feels so bad that he is not here with you. He's a good man, and he will wait for you and the baby. You must truly believe that Vanda.'

'Sometimes I feel like I'm living in Lalaland. All this business is just a dream, and I am going to wake up, and I will be sitting on the beach under the tower clock, and Egan will arrive, give me a kiss on my cheek and tell me he loves me.'

'Ah, if only that were true! I would gladly take all this away from you.'

Marco tapped on the bathroom door.

'Josie, Patty's on the phone,' he said from the other side of the door.

Josie opened the door enough for her to put her hand through and take the phone from Marco. She handed it to me and at the sound of my voice Patty simply broke down.

'Vanda, I love you. I wish I were there for you, my sister.'

'I do too Patty. I miss you so much! I'm so scared.'

We hardly spoke. Instead, we listened to each other's hearts breaking with pain. The connection started failing as Patty and Liam were making their way to their destination in the bush somewhere in the middle of nowhere. It would probably be ages before we would be able to speak again. I gave the phone back to Josie, who set it on the cupboard top, stood up and rolled off some sheets of toilet paper so we could wipe away our tears and blow our noses.

'Have you given any more thought to the baby's name?'

'I looked through the book Tali gave me, but there are just too many to choose. Then I tried to find the female name for Egan and came up with nothing. Then I looked up the meaning of

Egan and found out that it means fire, so I looked for a girl's name starting with an E that meant fire too, and all I found was Edana. I don't like the name and just got irritated, so I left it.'

Marco tapped on the door again and said calmly from the other side that Minister Wade had arrived. I sensed that Marco had probably been standing outside the door most of the time, silently praying, silently crying, silently being our protector.

Josie left the bathroom after kissing me on my forehead and whispering, 'I love you,' before I sunk beneath the water holding my breath, remaining submerged for a few seconds.

Minister Wade was just what I needed that evening. When he spoke, he calmed my nerves and reassured me that I would have all the support I needed from so many families. Mostly, though, he helped me refocus on God for support and my future.

Chapter Twenty-Five

The little pink pill did nothing for me as I tossed and turned restlessly the entire night, trying to play out the scene I would have to face within a few hours. I knew I wasn't ready for miles to begin this new life that was lying ahead of me. Frustrated at the lack of sleep that I was getting, I got out of bed and went to the kitchen for some milk. Standing there with only the light of the fridge escaping the darkness, I had the urge to run. Run away from all this negativity and run away from this place that had made me such a different person. I wanted to run back to the time in my life when I'd first met Egan. I knew where I had to go to regain my sanity. Leaving a note for Josie and Marco, I sneaked out of the house and went to the tower clock on the beach. Here I knew I could unwind and think clearly, or at least as clearly as was possible.

It was still dark as the winter sun rose much later in the mornings, and there was not a single person nearby. The air was still and silent, only interrupted by the occasional waves breaking on the sand, then rushing back into the ocean; and the occasional car or motorbike that passed by. I stayed in my car rather than sit on the wall, and stared at the white foam on the water, moving and reforming into shapes as the current directed the liquid orchestra.

'God, please help me to understand why I have received this burden,' I prayed and pleaded over and over with God, to send me answers. I knew deep down in my heart that the answers would be get revealed to me in time and that then I would understand, but I did not want to be so confused anymore.

The sky lightened as the sun began to rise from behind the tall buildings indicating to me that it was time to go home and face the day.

What kind of day was it going to be?

As I was about to start the car, my phone rang. I thought it would be Josie but was pleasantly surprised when I saw the caller ID, and automatically my heart skipped in a million directions.

'Good morning, my love!'

'Egan, it is so good of you to phone, and your timing is perfect. I've been sitting on the beach since three this morning and was just about to go home.'

'Couldn't sleep I take it? Well, that's quite understandable. How are you feeling?'

'Confused, tired, more confused, and very anxious. I know what is going to happen but at the same time, I don't. If that makes any sense at all?'

'My love I want so much to be with you. I know it won't take the inevitable away, but at least, I could hold you. I'm sorry, I am sorry that I am not there.'

The tears found their way down my cheeks unwittingly. I couldn't believe I still had tears left to waste.

'It is what it is,' I said, coughing out the lump in my throat before speaking, 'please just keep your phone near you today.'

'It will be in my hand the whole day. Phone whenever you want to. Vanda, I do love you, and somehow soon we will be together again, that I do promise you.'

'It has to be very soon okay. I love you so much too.'

The sun was above the car now, telling me I had to leave.

When they saw me walk into the house, Josie and Marco were in the kitchen trying very hard to hide their relief and trying very hard to be brave for me.

In a matter of two hours, we were at the hospital in Dena's room. Minister Wade and Jackie arrived not long afterwards. I was pleasantly surprised by the number of messages I was receiving from all my friends, including Glenna and her husband, Joe. I even got a message from Tali, which I appreciated. A message I would have loved to receive was from Patty, but I knew she did not have any signal. Still I longed to have her next to me.

I bent over Dena's motionless body and whispered in her ear, 'Hi Mom, please wake up, this is your last chance. You have to wake up now. Please, Mom.'

The baby moved as soon as I spoke and it sent a very strange sensation through my body, I couldn't quite explain it. As soon as I put my hand on Dena's stomach again, the baby kicked viciously.

'Josie, look!' I said quickly.

Josie looked at Dena's stomach jerking rapidly. She and Jackie both put their hands on Dena's tummy and smiled as they felt the tiny feet of this unknown human move against their touch. Dr Preston walked into the room and ruined the moment. He brought with him a bunch of nurses and an eerie air of death.

We all went to his consultation room and went through the procedure for the morning once more. He gave me several papers to sign, which I did, but with a lot of difficulties because my hand was shaking so much.

Before we left the office, Minister Wade gathered us in a circle. He said a final prayer for Dena and also prayed for a healthy baby, for the expertise of the medical staff and especially for strength for Josie, Marco and me. Marco went back to the room to say goodbye to Dena, and then he, Minister Wade and Jackie went to the waiting room.

Josie and I went to a room where we were giving blue gowns, booties and caps and were told to scrub our hands and arms before we entered the theatre. We made light of our appearance and the hospital fashion, which eased the tension only slightly. The doors opened, and we stepped slowly into a large, brightly lit, unfeeling theatre. A cold slab stood beneath a huge light in the centre of the room. Knives, scalpels, scissors and other instruments were laid out on a tray next to the slab. Machines surrounded the head of the slab, and I shivered, adjusting to the cold air and mood of the room. I could see the fear in Josie's eyes and for a moment that instinct to run came alive again. If it were not for the hold Josie had on my hand; I sometimes wonder if I might have done just that.

A loud bang gave us both such a fright that we jumped, as the main doors swung open and Dena entered on another mobile slab that was pushed alongside the centre one. The medical staff efficiently transferred her from the one slab to the other. Green sheets laid across her in such a manner that her tummy was exposed. A screen was positioned over her so that we could not see her belly once we stood at the top of the slab next to her head. The machines bleeped furiously, and my heartbeat thudded in the same rhythm. Josie and I held onto each other tightly, watching curiously as the medical staff swiftly and efficiently did what they were trained to do.

Dr Preston walked in, swinging the doors wide open, letting them bang shut behind him. He walked over to Josie and me, his hands held up high as he took great care not to touch anything, and he made sure we were doing okay so far. Neither of us had any words in reply; we could only nod our heads, still clinging to each other. Suddenly I was filled with panic.

Breathing was eluding me, and my entire body broke out in a cold sweat. My head wanted to explode, and I knew I was not going to be able to get through this.

'Josie, Josie,' I stammered, swaying ever so slightly.

'No Vanda, no, don't panic, it's nearly over, and I'm here. Vanda, hold on, be strong,' Josie said, shaking my arm, shaking the strength back into me, shaking the blood back into my brain so that I wouldn't faint, shaking me back into that cold room of death.

I stared around, dazed, and Dr Preston and all the staff looked worriedly at me. Josie nodded at Dr Preston. Dr Preston gave the word, and the staff took their places next to the slab. They all did their final checks and then the anaesthetist gave the final okay. Dr Preston picked up a shiny silver instrument, and I heard the sound of flesh being sliced open. I felt as though I was going to be sick. I saw Josie go white as a sheet and turn to me with the same stricken look that I imagined was on my face. We turned away from each other and looked at Dena's face instead. Still in her last minutes, she was breathtakingly beautiful.

The anaesthetist was watching both of us closely and kept reassuring us, at the same time constantly glancing at the machines and the numbers on them, and then checking Dena's face purely out of habit.

It was a matter of seconds, and a tiny sound became a shrill cry, so loud that it took over from the bleeping sounds of the machines.

'What a beautiful baby girl,' a nurse said as she wrapped the baby in a pink sheet and handed her to me.

Me?

I just looked at her frozen. I didn't want it. I didn't want to hold that baby. It wasn't mine. I couldn't shake off my frozen state. I couldn't tell my arms to reach out and take the baby girl from the nurse. That is what I was supposed to do. My brain knew it, but it wouldn't give my arms the instructions. I wouldn't take the baby. Josie took the baby and held her gently. She stood next to me trying to get me to hold her. She even went so far as to lift my arms in an attempt to put the baby in them.

'NO, NO!' I yelled stepping backwards, fixing my arms to my sides, but horrified at my reactions.

The nurse took Josie and the baby to the cot, and they did whatever it was they had to do. I heard them conversing with each other, without listening to what they were saying. I remained riveted to the spot. Unaware of what was happening within in the walls of the theatre, unaware of the movements, the conversations and the instructions being given and acted out. I stared only at Dena's cold, pale and lifeless face. There was no recognition in her eyes, no acknowledgment.

Was that even Dena lying there?

An arm gently rested on my shoulders and jilted me out of my state of shock and panic.

'Hey, Vanda, hey, it's okay now, it's all over.'

'Jo...Josie, Oh Josie! I'm so scared.'

'Come on now, let's go home.'

'No please, I must say goodbye to Dena, please.'

Dr Preston took my hands in his and softly and compassionately rubbed them.

'We will be switching the machines off now, Vanda dear. If you would like us all to leave and give you a few moments alone with your mother that would be fine. Once you're ready to leave, we will take your mom back to the room.'

'Please, I want to say goodbye please,' I spluttered.

'You want me to stay with you?' Josie asked, still holding me and caressing my arm with love.

Dr Preston nodded at the medical staff, and they instinctively left the room. Josie gave me a hug that lasted so long and was so tight that I felt the sobs breaking from her body against mine. She let me go, bent down and kissed Dena on the forehead and ran out of the room, tears streaming from her eyes.

I stood rooted to the spot next to Dena while Dr Preston moved over to the machines. He looked at me for confirmation. I could read the sympathy in his eyes; this was a part of the job he would rather not do. My body shaking and shivering, I managed to nod at Dr Preston, and he pressed the switch.

The room fell silent for a moment, the bleeps I had become so familiar with – I heard them even when I wasn't at the hospital – stopped with a final longwinded bleep. In the utter silence, one bleep startled me as it suddenly continued. I'd expected all the bleeping to end. I looked at the machines and noticed that the only machine still on was the one monitoring her heartbeat. I guessed that too would be silent soon enough.

'All done dear,' Dr Preston said as he hugged me lightly and disappeared from the room.

It was just Dena and me. The green sheets were still covering her body as she lay silent, the colour of death washed over her face.

'Mom, why? How can I raise a child, your child? Why Mom?'

My shoulders shook violently, the rush of tears, sobs and cries of despair running through and out of my body. I could not stand any longer and fell over Dena's body, shaking her, begging her to wake up – to wake up and give me back my life. I suddenly straightened as I realised the machine had missed a bleep. I stared at the machine. It made another bleep and then another and then another, and I felt relief. For a second, I thought I had killed her. My horror, my panic, my fears all collided at the sound of a bleep that did not end, and the machine had a long white line running across the screen.

'NO NO NO NO NO!' I didn't know what to do. I turned to run, I turned back to face Dena, turned to run again and turned back to Dena.

'NO NO NO PLEASE WAKE UP! WAKE UP!'

Dr Preston and several medical staff came rushing into the room.

'I think I killed her! NO! NO! NO! I killed her, I, I…I was shaking her!'

'No dear, that wouldn't have killed her. Remember I told you she would pass away soon after we switched off the machines. It's over now dear.'

Josie came running into the room and held me and led out of that room of death. Marco and Minister Wade and Jackie were all waiting to comfort and help, but I wanted none of it. I wanted the image of that room of death, of Dena's beautiful face of death, of the sound of that final never-ending bleep, to go away. I wanted to scream, cry, yell, shout; I wanted to hit something or someone it did not matter which. I wanted to run away; I wanted to get out of this nightmare. I couldn't be here. I had to go somewhere, anywhere, anywhere else but here.

Chapter Thirty-Six

Egan listened as I explained through my tears and a lump in my throat so large that it was almost impossible to form a word, my account of the birth and death that I had witnessed within minutes of each other. I could hear the pain in his voice and see the tears and the concern on his face through my laptop screen. I could see the guilt on his face for not being there with me that was so evident and expressed by every word he uttered.

'Soon we will be together, and we will start our forever. It can't be long now,' he repeated over and over again, finally convincing me that the worst was behind me.

I was back in the dreadful hospital with the memories of the previous day still so fresh in my mind. I stared at the baby sleeping peacefully in the incubator, trying with all her might to gain the correct weight. With the help of medication to survive, she tried with all her might to win me over. Josie reached through the armholes and stroked her legs. They twitched. They looked like sticks peeking out of the diaper – which was miles too big for her. It looked like extra skin had been wrapped untidily over her bones, and with each touch of Josie's hands, the little legs stretched out straight into the air, her tiny feet pointing toward the top of the incubator. She was so small; she looked like a little toy stuck in the middle of the sheet for decorative purposes until you noticed the pipes and tubes leading from her to the machines next to her.

'Touch her Vanda,' Josie said, trying to encourage me to put my arm through the peephole.

'No,' I replied defiantly and moved backwards.

At the mere thought of holding her, I went into panic mode.

How will I ever cope?

Dr Preston walked into the room with another doctor, a woman.

'Good morning ladies, this here is Dr Reddick, she is taking great care of this little lady here,' he said as he looked over at the baby, a smile on his face.

We introduced ourselves and shook hands and while De Reddick examined the baby, Dr Preston, caring as always, inquired as to how I was doing. All I did was shrug my shoulders. If I uttered a word I knew I would burst out crying, my eyes were already welling up with unwanted tears.

He placed a hand on my arm and said, 'She is beautiful, and she will be fine. All she needs is your love to get strong.'

I simply could not hear those words; it gave fuel to the anger I was trying so hard to control within me.

'Then her mother should have lived.'

Then I ran out of the room. I wanted to scream at anything and anyone. I wanted to hit the walls and throw the trolleys at anything within throwing distance - I wanted to cry, I wanted to pull my hair out, I was so angry, I wanted to curse the world. I reached my car, got inside and slammed the door shut, finally letting out the screams fighting to be released. Curses spilled from my lips, and I let out one after the other until I had no more air in my lungs. Then I relented to sobbing; huge blubbering sobs, uncontrolled sobs, wracking sobs, I poured out all my anguish, pain and confusion.

Why? Why? Why?

I held onto the steering wheel thinking that maybe I could just start the car and ride away and never turn back. But I knew I could not do that. I knew that for me to walk back into that ward I had to find the strength to force myself, and to look at the baby that looked so much like Dena.

Josie slid into the passenger seat and without saying a word she held me, her tears mingling with mine, sharing my pain, sharing my heartache, sharing my fears.

'When you're ready to come back inside and speak to Dr Reddick. She is very helpful but only come when you're ready.'

'Please stay with me, I can't go back in there alone.'

'I'm not going anywhere where you are not. We should first go to the bathroom though and wash our faces methinks.'

She smiled through her tear stained face, and I could not help but smile back.

Dr Reddick was staring at an x-ray placed against a lit screen. She turned around when she heard us approaching and smiled, gesturing for us to sit in the chairs near her desk. She was elderly and friendly, clearly very experienced in her field, and when she spoke her voice was uncharacteristically gruff. I was taken aback for just an instant as with her soft features I'd expected a sweeter voice. Still, though it was gruff, it was filled with concern and gentleness. We spoke for several minutes about what was expected of the baby and me, and what the procedures would be for the next few days. I heard but did not listen, still too emotionally drained and her words just bounced off my brain. She would simply have to repeat it all to me another time. We stood up and walked over to the incubator again. She opened the lid and took the baby out, handing her to me. I couldn't and stepped back instinctively, a look of utter horror on my face.'That's Okay; you need not be afraid. Take your time.'

Josie took the baby; it was so natural to her, the tiny human lay in her arms and squirmed a little, and then she cried for a short time - her cry was so young, so immature, and so new.

After a week of the same routine every day – get up, go to the hospital for an hour or so, listen to what the doctors have to say, come home and do it again in the afternoon and the evening – I was exhausted, even though I did not do much. In between this routine the funeral for Dena was arranged by Minister Wade and was held at the funeral home. A handful of people attended, as expected. The service was short, simple and to the point. There was no point elaborating on someone no one knew well. I could not find the energy to shed a tear but rather, was relieved when it was over. I thought I would be angry again, but relief overshadowed the anger instead.

On a rainy, very cold winter's morning, Josie and I left for the hospital, both dressed warmly in boots, jeans, polo neck jerseys, and thick wool-lined jackets. Our surprise awaited us in the ward when we saw the baby in a cot, dressed in a pink baby grow without any pipes or machines attached to her. She lay there happily chewing her hands, a pretty pink colour to her cheeks. She looked as though she had doubled in weight overnight. Dr Reddick smiled at our expressions.

'We wanted to surprise you. She can go home tomorrow, provided she has another stable night tonight.'

Josie giggled with glee and rushed over to pick her up. I just smiled or rather attempted a smile. Up until now I had not had to take any responsibility for her, as the medical staff and Josie had done everything. But now it would mean I would have to take care of her. And I did not want that. Josie tried once more to give the baby to me but once more I back-pedalled, making the excuse that I would hold her once she was at home.

I knew I was only prolonging the inevitable.

Egan was so excited the she was finally coming home, and he could finally get to see her. I found it so difficult to share in his excitement when I hadn't even held her yet.

'Don't worry love, when you do, it will be perfect.'

I wondered how he could be so confident. I certainly wasn't.

All night I wrestled with dreams of dropping her, burning her with bath water that was too hot or with her milk that was too hot, that she would hate me for not wanting her. It moved me to the point of waking up in a cold sweat, my heart pounding, and finally I got down on my knees and cried while I prayed more seriously than ever before. I had to give all my fears and worries to God. I had to ask Him to please take them away from me to help me be a mother to this child. To accept what was laid down before me and to allow Him to guide me. I had to do His will and not mine.

Josie and I packed a small bag with a pretty pink outfit for her to come home in and diapers and formula just in case. As it was so cold, we also packed a beanie and a thick warm blanket. 'Jeepers she is so small, and yet she has so much luggage,' I uttered matter-of-factly.

It was a Saturday, and much to Marco's delight he was able to come along to bring her home. We set off in the pouring rain, a car seat already installed in the car.

Arriving at the hospital's paediatric ward, and greeted by the entire medical staff that had all had a part in taking care of her since the birth. Her cot was smiling with pink balloons, and the teddy bears that she had received from so many kind and caring people. Once Josie had her dressed in her pretty pink outfit, many photos had been snapped and all the gifts, flowers and balloons had been taken to the car, we were ready to leave. I felt my heart begin to thump with anxiety and silently took a deep breath and said a quick prayer. I was grateful for God's quick response as I felt myself relish the calm flowing over me.

It was a dash to the car from the hospital as the rain pelted down with more force than when we had arrived. Marco drove slowly and ever so cautiously all the way home.

Josie put the baby in the cot as she'd slept through all the excitement, and while we both watched her sleeping, Marco carried everything in from the car, then joined us in watching her.

He put his arms around us both, 'She is beautiful Vanda, you are going to love her you'll see I'm right, just don't be scared. We are here always.'

I patted his hand. 'I know.'

'She needs a name hey,' he said, lifting her petite little hand into his large manly fingers.

I swallowed.

'The other night I couldn't sleep and that she did not yet have a name was bugging me. I started searching for Irish names on Google and came across Keela which means "a beauty only poetry can capture" – and I thought of her and of how beautiful she is, just like a poem. Her second name is Josiegan, a combination of Josie and Egan.'

Marco and Josie were silent, but I could see the tears trickling from Josie's eyes, and I could sense the emotions stirring in Marco. We all stood mesmerised by the beautiful baby girl sleeping peacefully and contently before us.

'Keela,' Marco choked out softly.

Chapter Thirty-Seven

Egan was mesmerised as he gazed at Keela through the webcam, lying in her crib adorned with white and pink material and her pink blanket. If it were possible for him to touch her through the screen and hold her, he would have. He ordered me to place the laptop next to her in the crib, and when satisfied he was as close to her as cyberspace deemed possible, he sang a most affectionate Irish lullaby he'd written especially for her. The strumming of the guitar was soft and gentle, as was his voice. I sat on the bed watching him. I missed him; I missed him so much.

When his parents were finally allowed to see Keela they were equally in awe of her, 'oohing' and 'aahing' when she moved a hand or pulled her mouth down to the sides. Her pure white skin was almost pink, and she had a mop of blonde hair and perfect rosebud lips.

After a lengthy video call with Egan and his family, Keela was still asleep, and I took the time to relax in a deep bubble bath, scented, as always, with lavender. Josie had done the same thing, and I can't say I blamed her at all – the last few weeks had been so exhausting. While I soaked up the water, I prayed that when Keela woke up, I would not panic as I had done every day since her birth. She was still sleeping when I returned to the room, and I quietly crept into my bed and curled up, wrapping myself in the covers. Josie said she would need to be fed at about eight o'clock, so I had, at least, an hour for a nap before then. I couldn't sleep though and just stayed warm under my covers thinking and worrying about whether I would be able to do this. Would I be able to hold her? Would I be able to feed her properly? Would she eventually love me? Would I love her?

They say the mother instinct kicks in naturally the second the baby is born, but I was not her mother, and I had not yet held her. I could only pray that somehow, and sometime soon, I would develop a similar instinct. She began to move around, and I remembered Josie telling me that this was a sign that she would wake up soon because she was getting hungry. I had her bottle and diapers all ready just like Josie had instructed me. I thought I should pick her up and try holding her before she started crying but I would probably panic.

I had to do this without Josie.

I stood over the crib for a few seconds watching as she squirmed and wriggled, it was amusing how she brought her bum up as she tucked her legs in underneath her tummy.

I took a deep breath, 'Oh please let me do this Lord.'

I reached out towards her, tucked my hands under her arms with my fingers extended behind her neck and head, just as Josie had shown me, and I lifted her up. She was wobbly and soft, like a stuffed toy. Her arms jolted open, and I immediately wondered if I had done something wrong, and I was about to put her back in the crib when she relaxed.

Maybe this was normal!

She opened her eyes briefly as I moved towards the bed, stepping ever so carefully and slowly, afraid of tripping over my own feet or of bumping into the crib. Gently, as though I was handling a fragile vase, I laid her down on the bed. She squirmed again, opening her eyes again and flinging her arms out. I crept into my bed again, getting under the covers hopefully without disturbing her too much. I quickly puffed up my pillows against the headboard to make a comfortable backrest, took another huge breath and picked her up as I had done before.

So far, so good!

I held her so that she rested on my forearms, remembering to support her neck. As she faced me her eyes opened, focusing on the dim bedside light as I gazed back at her, she was so beautiful, so perfect, and so tiny. Her outfit, even though it was a newborn size, was still miles too big for her. Leaning back against the pillows and carefully bringing her towards me until she rested against my chest, I eased my arms from around her, my body releasing its tension as I relaxed. I breathed out all the nervous air from my lungs. And then – oh my, oh my – the overwhelming feeling that I experienced I could not describe. Where it came from I will never know. I melted as Keela reached into my heart. I felt chemistry, love, a bond, a wave of emotions, a connection as our hearts joined. Was this the love a mother felt for her child when it was born? How could I ever find the words to describe this sensation, what my heart was feeling? All different sorts of emotions were rushing through my soul. I wanted to cry and laugh at the same time. I had never expected this, and I had no way of knowing how to deal with it. I shifted Keela so that her head nestled into my neck and I snuggled up to her, my head resting softly on hers. I was in love, and this love was like no other, this love was pure, genuine and it made me feel complete.

We lay together for what felt like forever. Forgiving and consoling each other, until Keela finally decided she was hungry, and she squirmed and wriggled letting me know that that was enough loving for now; now it was time to eat. As the seconds went by, she became hungrier and more restless, and when finally I had the bottle ready for her she sucked at it in such haste that she had gulped all the milk down in no time.

I burped her just as Josie had shown me and she certainly did burp – huge loud burps, very unladylike for such a tiny girl. When I had changed her diaper and put her into a clean babygrow, also as Josie had shown me, we resumed our snuggling position. The love was confounding and beyond overwhelming; it was incredulous to say the least. I sent a photo of the two of us positioned as we were to Egan, and it wasn't seconds later when my phone rang. I tried to explain as best I could to Egan what had just transpired and how much I wished he was with me to experience this moment. I told him I would pray that he would feel the same way when he finally met Keela. Egan assured me he would, and was relieved and overjoyed that I had finally overcome my fears, and even possibly my anger toward Dena. He told futuristic stories of our life together in Ireland, and I too saw our happy family. A few more months and we would turn our dreams into reality. I wanted it so badly I could taste it.

I woke up a few hours later to a face so lit up and smiling – it was Josie looking down on me.

'What a beautiful picture.'

'Josie, it was so amazing! I thought I wouldn't be able to do it, and then all of a sudden, there was all this love, and everything was just so right and so perfect.'

Josie took Keela off my chest, who hardly stirred when Josie cuddled her.

'So you told your mommy to get over it didn't you?'

My heart skipped a few beats at the sound of the word mommy.

Then I chuckled with glee, 'Mommy – well, let's just hope I don't have Dena's gene pool.'

'You will never be like Dena, Vanda. For one, you have a heart of gold, and two, you have God. And three, you have me that will give you a smack if you become anything like her.'

I hadn't felt so good waking up in such a long time. While we had coffee, I told Marco and Josie again and again of my experience. I simply could not get over it. When Keela started waking up, I went to her naturally, still slightly nervous but willing and eager.

While Josie cradled Keela in her arms and fed her, I thought of Patty missing out on this precious time in our lives. And of how happy Josie would be when one day Patty brought home her pride and joy; what a day of rejoicing that would be.

Chapter Thirty-Eight

For a few days, I thought this was the easiest job in the world. Keela slept and ate and was the most gentle and content baby any mother could've wished for until everything changed.

At approximately five o'clock every afternoon, Keela would scream blue murder. Josie and Glenna informed me that she was a colicky baby but that she would outgrow it eventually. Eventually when?

Each day as five o'clock neared I would grow anxious and pray that today would be the day it would end and that Keela would enjoy her bath and her food and be the happy contented baby she was those first few days.

It was not to be that day.

The plan to move back to my cottage had been put on hold until this colic stage was over. I was just not yet confident enough to take care of Keela on my own. Josie was wonderful and patient with me, even more so than with Keela.

Most mornings it was with such an effort that I got out of bed to go to work, the interrupted sleep every night was not boding very well with me at all. With a foggy mind focused on Keela and work, I still had to get my plans for Ireland together. I felt guilty for leaving Josie and Marco – they were my parents, and I was their daughter even if not by blood – and there would still be no contact with Patty for another month or so. With Keela being so difficult I had decided, and Egan had no choice really but to agree, that I would wait until she was over her colic before I made the journey. Another delay in the way of our forever, and sometimes it felt as though it was and always would be just a dream.

Egan spoke to Keela every evening, telling her stories of the car races in Ireland and their respective drivers and teams. If it weren't for his daily babbling to Keela, I would have completely forgotten about the world of cars. As much as I wasn't interested, in a strange way, I missed it. I missed going to the races with all our friends. I missed listening to all the lads talking about cars. I missed seeing Egan's face light up whenever a car got mentioned or how excited he became at the thought of going to a racing event.

I missed him.

On weekends I felt a little bit more like my old self, being among my friends, laughing, smiling and having conversations that were about girl things and not business or baby related. Katrin and Tania often visited me, and the house seemed to have a constant flow of friends visiting from the church. Other times we would all meet at the mall for a girls' day out, and it was these moments when I felt like myself again – even if I was pushing a pram. Jackie and Tali often visited during the week, and Tali always brought Coco along. Little Coco was fascinated by Keela and was always thrilled when I allowed her to hold her.

At church, Coco would be waiting for me to arrive, eagerly standing by as I placed Keela into the pram so that Coco could push her around to visit all the members and all the other little children. It was so sweet to see how the other children spoke to her, how they told her what was going on in their world and how they asked over her wellbeing. I was sure that Keela understood them better than she understood me.

Minister Wade, as always, was concerned and always asked how I was coping and offered his assistance wherever possible. He took me to one side while everyone was enjoying refreshing drinks after service and asked when I would dedicate Keela to God. Just the thought of having to stand in front of the whole congregation sent shivers down my spine, and so we agreed to discuss it after Bible study in the week. I felt saddened that I would have to do it alone. Since first becoming aware of the occasion where I'd dedicate Keela to God, I imagined it would be as a family, Egan included. Not just me, the single mother praying she was doing something right. When Minister Wade's attention was distracted by his daughter, I was left alone to ponder on these thoughts. I felt depressed, and a pang of anger nipped at my nerve ends. I knew I had to get out of there. I found Josie and convinced her we should leave. She went to find Marco and likewise I went to look for Coco to rescue Keela. Marco and Josie were sympathetic to my feelings rather than trying to play them down.

At home I was restless – not wanting to do anything but at the same time looking for something to do, and all I landed up doing was annoying myself. Standing at the edge of the pool I stared into the bright, clear blue water and I knew where I needed to be. It was time to introduce Keela to the tower clock, and, with a few bags packed and her stroller and my phone, we took a drive to my favourite spot on the beach. On such a fabulous day I knew it would be busy, but I still hoped I could show Keela where the best place in the world was.

The beach was overflowing with people and peppered with umbrellas, games, cooler bags and anything else to make it a perfect day. I had to park some distance away, and passers-by hindered the walk to the tower clock. Eventually, I found an area nearby the tower clock where I could comfortably set myself down on the sand, put my umbrella up and sit in peace for the rest of the day. The noise and bustle of people and cars went by unnoticed, as the sea intoxicated my mind and Keela lay sleeping next to me in nothing but a vest and her diaper. I thought of nothing as I stared at the ocean. Even the stream of people going in and out of the water and shrieking in the waves did not deter my thoughts from nothingness.

My mind was so far away, so far in a vast universe of blank, that I had not realised how far the sun had shifted and left my body exposed to its bright rays. The sound of Keela stirring in her chair brought me back to the present and the awareness of my burning skin. I looked at my arm and could immediately see how red it was. It couldn't have been in the sun for very long, but it had obviously been long enough. As I took Keela out of her chair and laid her gently on the picnic mat, I told her all about the tower clock and how it always made me feel sane amongst all the confusion in my life. She did not seem very interested; all that seemed to matter for the immediate moment was the grumbling in her tummy. The little cooler bag kept her milk fresh and cool, and she gulped at it almost desperately. I felt bad and wondered if she was not thirsty from heat rather than hunger.

Was I such a bad mother?

I looked around while I held her in my arms and she drank her milk, and I noticed a couple of other small babies sheltered from the sun under forgiving umbrellas.

Perhaps I wasn't!

Once Keela had her diaper changed, a fresh vest and her sunhat on, I took her to the tower clock and stood by it for a while. I was sure the people nearby thought I was crazy just standing in front of it, pointing to it and talking to Keela. She stared at the tower clock with squinting eyes, not used to the bright sun, and maybe I just imagined it, but I think she understood. We stood and watched young lads playing volleyball, memories of that summer with Egan flooding through me.

It seemed like a lifetime ago.

It seemed like it had been someone else's life, and not mine.

I went down to the water's edge to stop my mind from wandering down that depressive road, and I sat down in the sand. My boardshorts immediately absorbed the water, and I seated Keela between my legs so she – and her diaper – could feel the water moving as the tide pushed and pulled the water underneath us. At this new sensation, her little body shook with fright, and she let out a cry. I lifted her and gently placed her back in the same position until she eventually got used to the water.

As the sun began to slide closer to the edge of the ocean, I knew we would soon reach the horrors that five o'clock brought with it. It would be best to get Keela home before the people on the beach saw her other side.

At home, I sent Egan the photos I'd taken of the two of us at the tower clock and asked if he knew what was missing. He offered several possibilities; like, the rest of her clothes, the moon, my sunhat and so the silly list went on until he thought he had teased me long enough. I could hear the longing in his voice just as much as he could hear it in mine.

Keela let out a loud shriek, and I knew what time had arrived – the worst time of the day that lasted, at least, three hours. When would five o'clock become a normal time of day again, when would it pass by unnoticed?

Chapter Thirty-Nine

Keela was now four months old and every person that mentioned how fast the time had gone, made me feel even more as though it was dragging. Every day without Egan, even after such a long time apart, seemed to grow longer.

It was Marco's birthday, and Josie had invited a small gathering of close friends over to celebrate the occasion. Like every other occasion, some happy and some sad, we chose to celebrate under the lapa in their backyard. Marco was thrilled with the gifts and love he was showered with, cherishing every minute like it was his last. But the biggest birthday present he could've possibly wanted was arriving in just a few minutes.

We heard a car stop at the gate, and when we looked for Marco and Josie, they were already waiting with open arms, ready to embrace their daughter and son-in-law. Patty and Liam had decided to come home for a few months before taking on their next mission somewhere in Africa. The joy and happiness this brought to Patty's devoted parents made everyone's hearts sing.

Although Keela was still a colicky baby, I was, at last, confident and capable of moving back into the cottage as a single mother until I left for Ireland. And with Patty home, I did not feel as guilty about leaving Josie and Marco.

'Let me look at this gorgeous child, oh Vanda, she is beautiful,' Patty said once we finally had a moment together.

Patty was such a natural mother, holding Keela as if she were hers and as though she was a mother herself.

She should have a child, not me; I thought as Patty cuddled Keela to her bosom and immediately fell in love with her.

'I still can't believe we have this angel in our lives.'

'Wait till five o'clock, and then your opinion of this little angel will change very quickly,' I said laughing.

'So are you still going to Ireland?'

'As soon as her colic is over. I don't want to travel with a screaming child. I am going to be nervous seeing Egan again after almost two years, and also about meeting his parents. If I have a crying baby in my arms, I know I won't cope.'

I sounded as though I was trying to convince Patty rather than stating my plans.

'Once you're back together it will seem as if you were never apart. You will have everything you've wished for.'

'I certainly never wished for a baby!'

Patty started laughing. 'But she's so beautiful! How could anyone not love her?'

She stroked Keela's hair, checked her fingers and toes and simply admired God's perfection.

'Do you love her like a mother?'

'Well, it took me a while; up until the first night, she was at home. Until I first held her and then it was like magic. I can't explain that bond, that connection I felt to her, so yes, I suppose I do.'

'And Egan?'

'Well, I have to put the laptop next to her every night so he can sing the lullaby he wrote for her, and all he talks about is when we will be a family.'

'And?' Patty asked, dragging the word out, knowing I was hesitant about Egan.

'It's been so long I can't help but worry Egan is not going to feel the same when I get to Ireland. And then I will have to come back home broken-hearted, and I don't know if I could handle that disappointment. I'm afraid I will blame Keela and resent her for ruining my forever.'

'I'm so sorry I haven't been here for you. You needed me as your sister, and I was gallivanting in the wilderness. It must have been so awful, what you went through.'

Tears rolled down Patty's face in pure sincerity. I knew she would've been with me were it possible, but what could she have done to change the outcome? I would never have allowed her to alter her life for Dena.

'Don't be Patty. The outcome would still have been the same, and your mom was with me every second. Please don't cry. Besides, you're here now, and we get to see each other before I leave.'

I felt tears on my cheeks as I hugged Patty. It felt so good to hold her again. I had missed her more than I had thought. We released our loving embrace and wiped our tears dry and then laughed at our emotional silliness, all the while Keela stared at Patty with wide eyes.

'So, still no sign of a baby from you? Josie is going to nag you so that you know; she has had a taste of granny-hood and it's stuck on her.'

We both chuckled knowing I was so very right about Josie.

'We have this next mission to do, and that will be for six months, and then when we get back we want to have a baby, but don't say anything to my mom, please. We want it to be a surprise for her when it happens.'

'Won't say a word, I promise.'

I felt sombre at the thought of Josie having a grandchild that was her flesh and blood. Keela would never have that joy of a genuine grandmother. 'Your mom is amazing. Honestly, Patty, I don't know how I can ever repay her and your dad for what they have done for me. I probably would have run away if it weren't for them. There were a few times I very nearly did too. It was very close.'

'I'm quite sure my mom doesn't expect you to repay her, you are as much her daughter as I am Vanda, you know that.'

I had no words.

It was best not to say anything for fear of crying again, and I knew that all the emotional scars from Dena would come rushing to the surface. Those scars had to remain buried and forgotten.

A gentle knock on the bedroom door halted our emotional reunion as Liam peered in from behind the door.

'Hello ladies, I'm interrupting I know, but too bad.'

He smiled, and Patty gushed, still so madly in love with her husband.

'There are some enormous-sized steaks on the fire ready for eating and I have not had one of those in a very, very, very long time, so I'm asking, no I'm pleading, please come now so we can eat.'

His smile was as huge as the steaks he was already devouring in his mind. Patty neither rested Keela in her cot nor relinquished her from her arms; both were content within each other's immediate space.

The evening was so pleasant, so relaxed, and so enjoyable, it felt like old times, but the only obvious missing link was Egan. As joyous as my heart was at having my best friend, my sister, back under the same roof, my heart grew equally saddened at Egan's absence. When he phoned me, I gave the phone to Liam without telling him who was on the other end. When Liam said hello we all heard Egan's surprised shouting down the line and they relished in an hour-long conversation.

I couldn't go home. I couldn't drag myself away from Patty. I needed, oh I so badly needed to have an all-nighter with her when we could chat about nonsense. It was difficult actually to remember when last we'd done that. But that would have been selfish of me, I knew that. I knew how much Josie needed to be alone with her daughter, to hold her, to catch up on everything that had happened in Patty's life in the middle of nowhere since Christmas. Never mind how much Marco needed to have his baby girl cuddled in his arms while he listened to her stories.

Tomorrow was another day.

Back in my cottage, Keela lay fast asleep on my chest, totally oblivious to my restless spirit. I felt that my life was a constant case of "there will be a tomorrow".

Keela farted, highly unladylike and it stank. Goodness me, it stank so badly. What could I do but burst out laughing and checked her diaper? No wonder it stank.

'The joys of being a mother,' I said to myself while I laid her down on the bed, got a diaper, wet wipes, bum cream and changed her. She hardly stirred; it had been a busy night for her being passed around and entertained by everyone.

As she curled up fast asleep with a clean and pleasant-smelling bum, I gazed at her through my sleepy eyes. She was truly beautiful; I would have to move past the pain of always seeing Dena in her beauty, but I was so in love with her already. It was still hard at times to grasp the idea that I was a mother; that this bundle of perfection, my daughter, was completely and utterly dependent on me. That we would love each other as mother and daughter ought to love each other, as God intended. I would make sure of that.

And then she farted again. No! How was this possible? I checked her diaper again, and again there dwelled the smelly reason. The joys of being a mother! I shook my head as I thought about how much I did love her.

Chapter Forty

Minister Wade always had a theme for the second Sunday of every month, and this month was "Purely White" Sunday. We were never too sure who made up the themes, but it was always amusing and great fun. Basically, we only had to wear white, but as it was my turn to arrange the flowers for the communion table I chose to use Arum lilies as they were white as well.

Keela was dressed in a pretty white princess-style dress with a pale pink ribbon around the waist and a pink butterfly clip in her hair. To match, she had on the cutest white frilly socks with white sandals. She looked like the princess she was meant to be unless she blessed with me another stinky diaper of course! When I was finally satisfied that she was perfectly ready, I put her in her stroller so she wouldn't find some way of messing on herself and I would have to start all over again.

I got into a white cotton knee-length summer dress with flat white sandals. Nothing fancy or stylish but, with a baby, comfort was top priority – something I had learnt very quickly during those first few weeks when Keela had come home from the hospital.

Before I loaded her and her bags into the car, I carefully placed the flowers and vase on the front passenger seat. The lilies wrapped in newspaper and the vase in a towel. Keela sat patiently in the stroller until I was ready to strap her into her car seat and then waited patiently again for me to pack the stroller into the boot of the car. Finally, I put the bags on the seat next to her, climbed into the car and drove off.

Who needs to go to the gym when you have a baby? I laughed to myself.

Everyone seemed exceptionally happy. I wasn't sure if it was the theme and that white had a happy effect on people, or whether it was just my imagination. As always, Coco eagerly waited for the arrival of Keela, all the other little children in tow. It was the same routine every Sunday. I arrived, put Keela in the stroller and Coco pushed her away to their adoring fan club. Coco looked gorgeous in a white dress, enhancing her dark complexion and curly black hair. She looked like a little movie star.

I made my way through the crowds of people chattering away outside, to the communion table on the stage inside. The church was empty. It seemed odd as there was always someone standing about talking to their spouse or their children or friends, and there were always children running in and out of the building. But I did not take much notice and thought it was because it was such a nice day and people would rather be outside in the sunshine. That was logical enough for me.

Josh came in, which made me feel silly for thinking anything was amiss. He fiddled with the sound system, checked the podium and took an interested look at what I was doing and then left. Even the men were all in white. Everyone had taken this Sunday's theme to heart. While I fussed about with the flowers, I was sure I heard music nearby.

'Probably Josh messing around with the sound system again,' I muttered to myself and carried on adjusting the lilies.

The music was soft and gentle, as though someone was singing with a guitar. 'Probably one of the lads wasting time,' I mumbled to myself.

I listened, tilting my head to one side as if it would help determine where the music was coming from, I looked back at the pews and still there was no one in the church building. It was void of people, and yet it was filled with love. I also just realised that Josh had closed the doors behind him when he'd left. That was strange, and when I thought about it, I hadn't seen Minister Wade or Jackie either, so perhaps that was why everyone was still hanging about outside.

The music continued soothingly, and as I strained my ears to hear where it was coming from, it steered me toward the back of the stage. Putting the flowers down on the table, still incomplete in their arrangement, I slowly walked toward the music, curiosity getting the better of me. Whoever's voice it was, was so caressing and he – I presumed it was a he – sang as if he was singing to tell a story, an invitation for me to join him. The caressing voice enticed me towards the sound.

I slipped behind the closed curtains and walked to the middle of the stage, looked to the right and listened intently. The sound was not from the right of the stage. Slowly I turned and tiptoed to the left. There was a room to the left where they kept stationery and all sorts of décor items; it was pretty much a storeroom. As quiet as I could be, afraid of disturbing the sweet sound that was so intoxicating, I went down the few steps and stood at the door. It was slightly ajar.

The voice mesmerised me. If I went in it would stop and would I ever hear it again? Maybe I should just stay outside the room and listen to the sounds that spoke to my heart. I closed my eyes while the voice sang to me. I felt guilty as if I shouldn't be there, that perhaps I was stealing someone else's love song.

As I listened and listened to the voice, absorbing the melody, I gasped. I took such a deep breath that the air sucked into my toes, and somehow I managed to push the door open.

I was breathless. Stunned. Speechless. Shocked.

How?

I opened my mouth to speak, but no words came out. My tears mirrored his tears as his made their way past that smile, that beautiful Irish smile that I'd missed and had longed for, for such a long time.

'About time you found me.'

I opened my mouth to speak again, but again the words eluded me. Egan stood up gently and placed his guitar on the stool. He walked toward me slowly, his eyes never moving from mine, as if seeking approval for his actions. He slowly reached out his hand to touch my face. The touch of his hand against my cheek had me shaking. It felt so perfect, exactly as I had remembered. I put my hand on his hand to make sure he couldn't escape. To make sure this was real, to make sure it wasn't a dream and that it really was my beloved Egan standing right before me, looking lovingly into my tear-filled eyes.

He pulled me towards him and kissed me softly, tenderly and lovingly on my lips. I felt all the blood drain from my face. My lips tingled with glee; they had waited so long for that kiss. Egan pulled away slowly, the sensation of his kiss lingering on my lips.

'Marry me.'

My eyes widened. I was stunned for a second before I could force my voice to speak.

'M...marry?' I stuttered.

Egan giggled, his Irish laugh spilling over my confusion.

'Marry me, please?'

My mouth made all sorts of shapes until I could finally form a single word. 'Yes.'

'Now, today, marry me, please.'

'Today, now?'

'My love, it has all been arranged. I phoned Minister Wade two weeks ago. All that had to happen was you had to say yes. I left Ireland yesterday with my family...'

'Family?' I interrupted.

Again Egan's face was covered by his smile. 'My father bought out my contract from the embassy; he said he couldn't stand my pain any longer. And they're all here, now, waiting for us to get married.'

I reached for his face, tracing his lips with my fingers.

'You're staying here? You're not going back?'

My mind was reeling.

'Nope my love, our family, our life, our forever will be here or wherever we want to be as long as you marry me.'

I flung my arms around him, holding onto him, hugging him to me, afraid to let go, and he wrapped his arms around me, equally desperate never to let me go.

'Keela! You have to meet Keela first.'

He kissed me again, this time, far more passionately until we were both out of breath. I felt my knees buckle beneath me from the spell he'd cast over me, but he felt it too and caught me and held me to him.

'Let's get Keela then.'

He put his arm around my waist, tugging me into him closely and I felt his heart beating as fast as mine. As we walked through the curtains, a burst of cheers and loud applause broke our spell. Everyone all dressed in white, all in on Egan's plan for our wedding ceremony. Egan led me down the stairs straight to his family who already had Keela in their arms. He introduced me, and warm, affectionate embraces smothered me. I stared in awe at the Irish lad beside me; our faces drenched in happiness and alighted with absolute love.

I woke up this morning feeling like it was just another day and now, a few hours later, my life had just begun. God heard and answered my prayers in His time.

When is my forever?? Now.

POSTSCRIPT

Giving my life to God and living as His servant did not mean my life would be without difficulties.

I allowed anger and disappointment to control my emotions, and they took priority in my life over God.

Anger cannot heal or fix a situation. Instead, it becomes a hindrance. It forces confusion and hatred and bitterness and blocks the path for God to do His work in our life.

There is not always an answer as to why there are traumatic experiences, sadness, death and hatred in our lives. We could spend a lifetime asking ourselves 'Why?' and never come to a conclusion.

Only God has the answers.

Life happens, but the question to ask is: With whom do you share your life?

Who is your pillar of strength?

Who, at the end of this life, gives life?

Will you live Forever in eternity?

<u>YOUR OPINION</u>:

You've come to the end of this story; I truly hope you enjoyed it and it touched your heart.

Please be kind and leave your review for the benefit of the many to follow, I will be so appreciative.

https://www.amazon.com/When-My-Forever-Aileen-Friedman-ebook/dp/B00BFP01CQ/

Thank you
God bless you

Aileen Friedman

MORE BOOKS BY THE AUTHOR

Aileen Friedman

Changes From a Sunset
ISBN 978-0-620-52564-0

Second is Best
ISBN 978-0-620-59758-6

The Sparkle in Her Eyes plus Six more Short Stories
ISBN 978-0-620-64434-1

The day God came to earth.
ISBN 978-0-620-68628-0

Radar Love
ISBN 978-1-543-29950-2

Mr. Trolley Adventurer
ISBN 978-1-533-27328-4

Jamie's Discoveries
ISBN 978-1-533-27339-0

The Secret of Grace
ISBN 978-1-719-17242-4